Shelley couldn't believe her ears.

'You heard,' Drew whispered softly. 'You've become one of those women who know the cost of everything and the value of nothing, haven't you, Shelley? Seems like I had a lucky escape.'

'Or maybe you just don't like the way I dress because the clothes I wear indicate that I'm an independent woman now?'

'Independent?' His lips curled like an old-fashioned movie star's. 'I don't think so! Being a rich man's plaything doesn't usually fall into the category of independent.'

Sharon Kendrick was born in West London and has had *heaps* of jobs which include photography, nursing, driving an ambulance across the Australian desert and cooking her way around Europe in a converted double-decker bus! Without a doubt, writing is the best job she has ever had and when she's not dreaming up new heroes (some of which are based on her doctor husband) she likes cooking, reading, theatre, listening to American West Coast music and talking to her two children, Celia and Patrick.

Recent titles by the same author:

ONE BRIDEGROOM REQUIRED!
ONE WEDDING REQUIRED!
ONE HUSBAND REQUIRED!

THE FINAL SEDUCTION

BY

SHARON KENDRICK

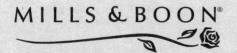

MILLS & BOON®

With thanks to Simon for beautiful Hillyard Boats and to John
for making Milmouth come alive! Oh, and a great big
'miaow' to Arthur at the Westover Hall.

DID YOU PURCHASE THIS BOOK WITHOUT A COVER?

If you did, you should be aware it is **stolen property** as it was reported
unsold and destroyed by a retailer. Neither the author nor the publisher
has received any payment for this book.

*All the characters in this book have no existence outside the imagination
of the author, and have no relation whatsoever to anyone bearing the
same name or names. They are not even distantly inspired by any
individual known or unknown to the author, and all the incidents are
pure invention.*

*All Rights Reserved including the right of reproduction in whole or in
part in any form. This edition is published by arrangement with
Harlequin Enterprises II B.V. The text of this publication or any part
thereof may not be reproduced or transmitted in any form or by any
means, electronic or mechanical, including photocopying, recording,
storage in an information retrieval system, or otherwise, without the
written permission of the publisher.*

*This book is sold subject to the condition that it shall not, by way of
trade or otherwise, be lent, resold, hired out or otherwise circulated
without the prior consent of the publisher in any form of binding or
cover other than that in which it is published and without a similar
condition including this condition being imposed on the subsequent
purchaser.*

*MILLS & BOON and MILLS & BOON with the Rose Device
are registered trademarks of the publisher.*

*First published in Great Britain 1999
Harlequin Mills & Boon Limited,
Eton House, 18-24 Paradise Road, Richmond, Surrey TW9 1SR*

© Sharon Kendrick 1999

ISBN 0 263 81820 9

*Set in Times Roman 10½ on 12 pt.
01-9910-49941 C1*

*Printed and bound in Spain
by Litografía Rosés, S.A., Barcelona*

CHAPTER ONE

As SOON as she heard him call her name she knew that something was wrong.

Very wrong.

'Shelley?'

Shelley frowned at the intercom. 'Yes, Marco?'

'Are you busy?' He spoke every word as if it were poetry. Sexy, deep, strong, lyrical. The kind of voice that drove women crazy. Shelley had seen it for herself, time after time.

Waitresses would go ga-ga for that voice. Female bank employees would flutter their eyelashes—even women who were old enough to know better started coming on to him like small-town hookers. Actually, they were the worst. Rich, confident, bored middle-aged women who fancied the idea of an Italian lover in their bed. And out of it!

Shelley wondered if he was being hounded by one of the more persistent females. It happened. Maybe that was why he wanted to speak to her—to ask her to let his pursuer know in the nicest possible way that he was definitely *not* available!

'No, I'm not especially busy.' She glanced down at the glossy catalogue she had been studying on his behalf. Marco was currently the hottest art dealer on the international circuit, and Shelley made sure he kept his crown by oiling the wheels of his life—so that it ran as smoothly as possible. 'What's up?'

'We need to talk.'

'I'm all yours, Marco.' She closed the catalogue and pushed it to the front of her desk.

'Good.' Seconds later he appeared at her door, almost as if he had been lingering outside in the corridor, like a person waiting to be interviewed.

Shelley stared at him. Something was different. 'Is everything okay?'

He hesitated, thick black lashes shading the ebony glitter of his eyes. 'I'm not quite sure how to answer that.'

She watched while he came into the dazzling light-filled room which she was lucky enough to call her office. Watched his air of distraction as he walked over to the window to gaze out at the lake beyond. The morning sun made the waters glitter and throw back the intense golden light—as if someone had scattered the surface with sequins.

He turned back to face her and, as always, Shelley derived intense pleasure just from looking at him. It was like looking at a beautiful painting or a perfect sky. She knew how lucky she was and how many people envied her—with her perfect job and her perfect boss.

'Shall I make us some coffee?'

He shook his head. 'No. Thanks.'

For the first time, she noticed the unfamiliar shadows beneath his eyes and deep in her subconscious little warning bells began ringing sounds of danger. Marco always slept like a baby. 'Something is wrong, isn't it?' she said.

He sat down opposite her and spread his hands expansively, in a very Italian way. 'Not wrong—just different. Something has changed.'

'Don't speak in riddles, Marco,' she implored. 'You know I can't stand suspense! I'm the kind of person who reads the reviews of films before I go to see them, just so I can find out the ending!'

'There is no easy way to say this, Shelley—'

And then she guessed. 'You've met someone?'

'Yes.'

'And you've fallen in love.'

'Yes, again.'

'It's obviously serious.'

'It… Yes,' he admitted, and for a moment his face looked almost severe. 'Yes, it's serious. Very serious.'

'Serious in that you've already shared breakfast in bed?'

'Shelley!' he protested, but he was smiling. 'How can you ask me such a question?'

'Because I'm a woman, and because I'm curious! Or did you imagine I'd find it painful?'

'I guess I did. Well, not painful exactly. Difficult.'

'Because I've lived with you for three years and every woman in Italy would like to scratch my eyes out because of that?'

'Shelley!' He hesitated. 'You know—if I could change things I would.'

'Fall out of love again, you mean?'

'No.' He shook his head. 'Rewrite history.'

'Well, you can't,' she said flatly. 'No one can.'

'But I took you away,' he said slowly, painfully. 'I took you from Drew.'

Drew.

His name washed over her like the morning tide.

She had seen him in her dreams so often—especially at the beginning, when everything was still so raw, and so painful. But it was a long time since either she or Marco had spoken that name aloud and, oddly, it hurt more than it should have done. Even after all this time.

Shelley shook her head, mainly to rid herself of the face which had swum into her memory with pin-point clarity. Sapphire eyes and honey-tipped hair. The body of a labourer, with the face of an angel.

'Please don't say that you "took" me, Marco!' she protested softly. 'It makes me sound like a piece of merchandise to be picked up at the supermarket—a can of beans!'

'But I did!' he gritted. 'You know I did!'

'And you certainly didn't take me from Drew!' she contradicted. 'That would imply that he owned me. And he didn't—even if he thought that he did. No one can own another human being, however much they try.'

'But you were engaged to him,' he pointed out gently. 'Weren't you?'

'I wore a cheap little ring on my finger!' she cried. 'A mark of possession—that's all engagement rings ever are! A metal circle which said "Keep off—she's mine! And I can do what I like with her because she wears my ring!"'

She blinked back the sudden and mysterious tears which had made her eyes go all blurry. She hadn't thought about that ring for a long time, but now she had more important things to think about. Like doing the decent thing and leaving as quickly as possible. Not standing in Marco's way. The way they'd always agreed. 'Can you arrange an early flight for me, Marco?'

'Of course. But where will you go?' he questioned quietly.

'Why, back to Milmouth, of course.' She gave him a gentle smile. 'Where else would I go?'

'It will be—painful?'

'Very probably,' she agreed. 'And difficult too, I expect. But Milmouth is my home. It's where I grew up. More importantly, I have a house there—and I'll need somewhere to live while I make up my mind what I want to do next.'

'You'll go and live there?' he breathed in surprise.

'You find that so strange to imagine?' she asked. 'Why—because it's a tiny little place compared to the near-palaces I've lived in with you?'

'I think you'll find that you've outgrown what you had there.'

'We'll see.'

'But more than that—aren't you forgetting the one big difficulty of going back there?'

She met his eyes, knowing what he meant, but needing to hear him say it. 'Like what?'

'Why, Drew of course. Drew still lives there, doesn't he?'

She shook her head. 'I don't know. I don't know what Drew does. I don't know anything about his life. Which is hardly surprising really, is it, Marco? I cut my ties with Milmouth a long time ago. And since my mother died there's been no one there to keep me up to date with what's happening. I'm too much of the bad girl and the black sheep for anyone to want to bother with me.'

He hesitated. 'I'll give you a breathing space. A month or so—before I make any kind of announcement.'

Her face showed her surprise as she rose to her feet, smoothing her sleek cream dress down over her narrow hips. 'You're going to make a statement?'

'Yes, I am.' His face was calm and serious. He looked happier than she had seen him look for a long time, but she was aware of the burden which hovered over his shoulders. 'I no longer intend living a lie.'

'Good.' She nodded. 'Me, neither.'

'Shelley?' The voice was lower now. Honey and stone. Soft yet forceful. Rich and deep. Once she had been unable to resist that voice, but she had been weaker then. And foolish. Now she was a woman, and she had grown. She had.

'Mmm?'

'I'm going to miss you.'

She gave him a smile which was more wistful than sad. *'I'm going to miss you, too,'* she said, and turned and walked out of the door, realising as she did so that it was the only time she had spoken in English during the entire conversation.

CHAPTER TWO

THE sleek grey car bumped over the dip in the road and Shelley craned her neck.

Just here. Here. If you looked really closely, you would catch your very first glimpse of the sea. Every time she had ever travelled this road it had been there to greet her, like an old friend.

She screwed her eyes up, making out the deep sapphire slash which contrasted against the paler blue of the sky. Beautiful. Why did the sea always look so blue from a distance even when up close it seemed murky and dull? She put her foot down on the accelerator and drove on.

The car was new and unfamiliar, just as the roads seemed unfamiliar—even though she knew them like the back of her hand. But it seemed strange to be driving on the other side of the road after Italy, towards a place which she had once called home. She hadn't been back since her mother's funeral, and that had been almost two years ago.

Two years. And things would have changed. She knew that. She was prepared for that.

The signpost for Milmouth pointed to the right but Shelley was headed straight on, where her mother's old house lay just beyond the cute part of the village. Just one of a small cluster of houses—simple, rather stark houses—whose main function had been to provide homes for the poorly paid workers of Milmouth.

She slowed the car down. It made more sense to go home first. She badly needed to freshen up and let some

11

air into a house she knew would be dusty with neglect.
But instead she found herself indicating right, curious to
see the small seaside town she had grown up in. The
house could wait, but Shelley couldn't. It had been too
long, and she needed to see the sea again and breathe in
the salty tang of the air which always made you feel so
alive.

Nearly three years away in all, and in that time she
had changed out of all recognition. Had the town changed
alongside her? Old buildings torn down and replaced with
shiny new ones? New families come to replace the ones
she'd grown up with?

The sun splashed golden patches over the green, giving
the place a curiously restful feel, and she eased the car
into a vacant parking spot just behind the war memorial.
There was scarcely a soul in sight. Still, it was Sunday
afternoon and not much happened *anywhere* on a Sunday
afternoon. Let alone Milmouth.

She got out of the car and locked it, thinking that it
seemed like a long time since Marco had turned her un-
troubled world upside down with his news, but the reality
was two days. Two days of cars and planes, delays and
a few major readjustments along the way.

Shelley stretched her arms and began to walk towards
the sea, passing a small boy clutching a football beneath
his arm, his father at his side. With big eyes, the boy
stared up at her as they walked past and she smiled back
at him.

'Who's that woman?' she overheard him asking his
father.

'Shh. I don't know. Don't stare, Michael. It's rude.'

Did she look that remarkable, then? She supposed that
maybe she did, in her linen suit and long leather boots—

more suited to the high-fashion city of Milan than to this tiny backwater of a place.

It was a brilliantly cold autumn day and the wind tugged at her short hair as she walked past the tidy houses with their immaculate gardens and shamelessly corny name-plates. Sea-View. Island-View. Ocean-View.

And then the wind became stronger—the light shining and brilliant in the vast sky—and Shelley drew in a long breath as she reached the pebbly beach and got her first real glimpse of the sea.

The platinum-blue waters were topped with palest, purest gold and in the distance a scarlet-sailed boat bobbed up and down on the metallic waters, looking like an illustration in a children's book. Directly ahead, the Isle of Wight lay crouched low in the water, like a sleeping cat. Although the island was four miles away, perspective tricked you into thinking it was closer and Shelley had spent many hours on the beach as a child, fruitlessly skimming stones towards it. Trying to hit the wretched thing!

Years later there had been moonlit parties on this same beach and later still, whipped by wind against the sea wall, Drew had first taken her into his arms and kissed her...

With only the mournful call of the gulls puncturing the rhythm of the waves, she stood staring at the water for ages, until a movement caught her eye and she slowly turned her head to look up towards the western shore.

The only activity was the dark shape of a man walking towards her, the pale blur of a dog frolicking beside him. Idly, she screwed up her eyes and watched them for a moment.

The dog kept running into the bubbling foam on the shoreline and then barking back to the man again, clearly trying to catch his attention. But the man remained oblivious, his head bent, deep in thought.

There was something terribly compelling about the duo and then Shelley found herself frowning with disbelieving recognition as they grew closer, her heart jerking painfully in her chest as suspicion became certainty.

Drew!

She shook her head. It was fantasy. She had magicked him up with her thoughts. She swallowed and looked away, then back again. He was almost upon her now and unmistakable, his long-legged stride effortlessly covering the distance, his head still bent as he crunched his way over the pebbles.

He still hadn't noticed her but the dog had, and Shelley felt her mouth drop open in disbelief. 'Fletcher!' she breathed, and whistled to him before she could stop herself.

The dog pricked its ears up and then came charging at her full-pelt. Shelley shrieked as a flurry of pale gold fur and scrabbling eager paws almost knocked her off her feet. 'Fletcher!' she protested weakly.

And then she did go down, slap-bang hard as her bottom hit the stones. Her breath was jolted out of her as the dog attempted to lash its rough tongue over her cheeks. 'Ow!' she yelped. 'Get off!'

'Duke! *Down*!' came a deep, furious command and the dog fell away immediately, dipping his head low and dropping his tail as the man approached. 'Get off her, Duke!' he yelled, and the dog, clearly unused to such a violent command, whimpered and slunk off to cower behind the wind-break.

Shelley blinked in confusion as she tried to catch her breath. *Duke?* She was winded, her legs sprawled out in front of her, the linen skirt riding high up her thighs as she gazed up into a pair of disbelieving blue eyes.

'Shelley Turner,' he stated flatly.

'The very same,' she whispered back, and braced herself for his reaction, unprepared for the soft venom which dripped from his voice.

'And which big, bad fairy brought you back into town, kitten?'

The 'kitten' bit was habit, but it still hurt. The first time he'd ever said it to her she'd felt as if she'd hit the jackpot. 'No fairy—bad or otherwise. Just a car,' she smiled, as though she confronted men like dark, avenging angels every day of her life!

'And what are you doing here?'

'You mean right now? I'm sitting on these damp pebbles getting my bottom wet!'

His face stayed stony, but he automatically put his hand out to help her up. 'Here!'

'Thanks!' She caught it. Her cold fingers seemed bloodless in his warm, calloused grasp and her breath was lost on the wind.

He bent and, with his other hand, cupped her elbow, so that he was able to swing her easily to her feet, but he didn't let go. Not straight away. As if he could tell that her knees were still too shaky to support her. He didn't speak again, either, just subjected her to a hard, silent scrutiny while she dragged the salty air back into her lungs.

She hadn't seen him since her mother's funeral—where he had stood in the shadows at the back of the church. He had been wearing a brand-new suit—the first time anyone in Milmouth could remember seeing him in a suit. He must have bought it specially. She had been moved by that. More than moved.

But they had hardly spoken—other than Shelley thanking him for coming, and him stiltedly saying that she knew how much he'd loved her mother. Which was true. And he had looked ill at ease. Not surprisingly. As if he had been dying to say something not very nice to her, but hadn't been able to as a mark of respect.

Ever unconventional, he had sent a big bunch of tiny pale mauve Michaelmas daisies, with their yellow centres glowing like miniature suns. Her mother's favourite flower. And when Shelley had seen those she hadn't been able to stop crying…

Now her heart drummed with the vibrant reality of seeing him again. It had been a long time—in fact it gave her a real jerk when she realised just how long it had been.

She stared at him.

A couple of the lines on his face weren't quite as faint as before. And the eyes had lines at the corners which had not been there before, either. Crinkly little laughter lines, which made Shelley wonder who had put them there. The hair was still thick, still ruffled—all dark and windswept with the ends lightened to honey by the sun.

He was taller than Marco—taller than nearly all the men she had ever met, and most of that seemed to be leg. His faded denims matched the sky, while the navy sweater matched his eyes.

Her first, instinctive thought was that she must have been mad to ever leave him. But that wasn't a very smart thing to think. You shouldn't wish for the impossible, and you couldn't rewrite history. And the unfriendly look in his eyes told her that he certainly wouldn't want to—even if you could.

'Hello, Drew,' she said at last, and with that he let her go. She half stumbled and she saw him tense as if to save her if she fell again. But she didn't. Just tottered for a moment on the too high heels of her leather boots. She smiled up at him, as anyone would in the face of such courtesy. 'Thank you for coming to my rescue.'

He didn't bother with any niceties. And he didn't smile back. 'Don't make me out to be Sir Galahad,' he drawled. 'He shouldn't have knocked you over. He knows he's not to jump up at people like that.'

'It was my fault.' She looked over at the dog and realised her mistake. The animal was paler and thinner and much younger than the dog she remembered. 'It isn't Fletcher?'

'How could it be?' he asked impatiently. 'Fletcher was almost crippled when you left—not jumping around like a puppy. I know they say that the Milmouth air is rejuvenating but that would be a little short of miraculous!'

'Still, I shouldn't have called him like that.'

'No, you shouldn't,' he agreed shortly.

'He's lovely, Drew,' she said, meaning it. 'When did you get him?'

'He isn't mine.' His eyes were wintry. 'I'm just walking him for somebody else.'

'Anybody I know?' The question came out before she realised that she had no right to ask him things like that.

He clearly thought so, too. 'What would you say if I told you I was out walking him for a sweet, little old lady?'

The trouble was that she would believe him. 'I'd say that you were a model citizen. An upstanding member of the community.'

'*Would* you?' he queried softly, and let his gaze drift unhurriedly over her face. 'Would you really?'

Shelley shifted. She was used to men staring. That was what men did in Italy. It was acknowledged and recognised as perfectly normal to gaze at a woman in open appreciation, as you would a fine painting, or a delicious meal. But the way Drew was looking at her was making her feel uncomfortable. As if she were some bit of flotsam he had found washed up on the beach.

And he was shaking his head, as though he didn't like what he saw. 'What on earth have you done to yourself?' he demanded in a low, incredulous voice.

He made her feel like Cinderella before the transformation scene. '*Done* to myself?' Her indignation was genuine. 'What's that supposed to mean?'

He shrugged. 'Well, the dog wouldn't have knocked you over if you hadn't been so damned skinny.'

'*Skinny?*' she gritted. The word was insulting—as he had obviously meant it to be. 'Don't you know anything, Drew? That a woman can never be too thin—'

'What a load of rubbish,' he interrupted with quiet, curling distaste. 'Haven't you heard that the waif look is out? You look like you haven't eaten a square meal in years.'

Should she bother telling him that women in Milan watched their figures like hawks? Which was why they looked beautiful and elegant in the wonderful fashions which the city was so famous for. 'Clothes look much better if you aren't carrying any excess flesh,' she told him smugly. 'Everyone knows that.'

'Well, I prefer to see a woman out of clothes,' he drawled, noticing with pleasure that she flinched when he said *that*. Good! He smiled as his gaze lingered in a way which was now *very* Italianate. 'And when a woman is naked a few curves are infinitely preferable to looking like a bag of bones.'

'Bag of bones?' she repeated in horrified disbelief,

feeling quite sick at the thought of him with naked women. 'Are you saying that I look like a bag of bones?'

He shrugged. 'Pretty much. You sure as hell don't look great. Mind you—' and his gaze narrowed '—the clothes don't help—and what on earth have you done to your hair?'

Shelley could hardly believe what she was hearing! She had learnt a lot about looking good while she had been living with Marco. From a rather wild and wind-swept girl, she had become high-maintenance woman. She had transformed herself from small-town hick to city slicker. People admired the way she looked these days—her hips were as narrow as a boy's and she only ever wore neutrals.

But Drew didn't seem to be one little bit impressed by her new-found fashion know-how.

She glanced down at her admittedly rather crumpled grey linen suit—and then back up into a pair of judge-mental navy eyes.

'I agree that this isn't what I would normally wear to walk on the beach,' she allowed. 'But this suit was de-signed by one of Milan's most desirable couturiers.' She saw him pull a face, and as the events of the last days took their toll something inside her snapped.

'Most women would give their eye-teeth to own an outfit by this designer!' she fumed. 'And as for my *hair*! For your information, it is shaped and tinted with high-lights and lowlights every six weeks, by one of Milan's finest cutters. Have you,' she heard herself asking inane-ly, 'any idea of how much it costs to look like this?'

But as soon as the words were out and she saw the look on his face she wished she could unsay them.

Distaste wasn't the word.

'I should have guessed that money would have been

at the top of your agenda! So no change there.' He gave a scornful little laugh. 'Well, for your information, kitten—you were done.'

'*Done?*'

'Yeah, done. Conned. Fleeced. Cheated.'

Shelley couldn't believe her ears. '*What?*'

'You heard,' he whispered softly. 'You've become one of those women who know the cost of everything and the value of nothing, haven't you, Shelley? Seems like I had a lucky escape.'

'Or maybe you just don't like the way I dress because the clothes I wear indicate that I'm an independent woman now?'

'Independent?' His lips curled like an old-fashioned movie star's. 'I don't think so! Being a rich man's plaything doesn't usually fall into the category of independent.'

She didn't have to defend herself to him, so why did she suddenly feel as though she was in the witness box?

She chipped the words out like ice. 'I virtually ran the art gallery in Milan, for your information!'

'What? Flat on your back?'

Shelley opened her mouth to snap back at him, but no words came. This wasn't how it was supposed to be. She had imagined seeing Drew again one day; of course she had. Every woman thought of the man they had almost married from time to time. And she had had lots of imaginary conversations with him inside her head. But they had been nothing like this. Rather, some of them had gone along the lines of him narrowing his eyes in appreciation and giving a long, low whistle while a look of profound regret would give his body a kind of *deflated* look, before he said something like, 'Wow!'

Others had been stupidly unrealistic versions involving

white lace and rice and confetti, but she had banished those very early on. They used to make her pillow damp with tears.

But not this. She met the mockery in his eyes.

'Actually,' she said, with acid-sweetness, 'while you've been busily hammering nails into pieces of wood, I've learnt to speak fluent Italian, as well as how to—' She looked pointedly at where the denim was at its thinnest, stretched tautly over his mouthwatering thighs. She swallowed. 'Dress.'

'Just not very attractively,' he amended silkily. 'Shelley, your arrogance is simply breathtaking.'

'Then it's a good match for yours, isn't it, Drew?'

'So where is he?'

She played dumb. 'Who?'

'Your lover, your mentor, your stallion—'

'Please don't call him that!'

'Why not? Does the truth offend you?' He looked around the empty beach with exaggerated scrutiny. 'I expect he's somewhere warm and comfortable, is he, polishing the leather of his hand-made shoes?'

'Why, you…you…*Philistine*!' Her eyes swivelled to *his* feet. He wore a scruffy old pair of canvas deck-shoes, without socks. *Without socks!* Marco would have sooner gone to prison than gone out in footwear like that! He would have said that those were shoes for a tramp. And yet somehow Drew managed to look nothing like a tramp. He looked, Shelley realised with a lurch of horror, he looked incredibly sexy…

'You look like you should be standing on a street corner begging for small change!' She glared at him.

His body tensed, as though he was fighting some dark, internal demon, and then he shook his head slightly. 'I guess we've traded all the insults we need to. Why don't you tell me how long you're here for, Shelley? Just passing through? Or have you come to put your mother's old house on the market?'

She didn't stop to think, but then maybe she didn't need to. Maybe she had known all along just what her answer to this would be. 'Why would I be passing through? Milmouth doesn't take you anywhere. No, I've come home, Drew,' she told him, observing his frozen reaction more with pain than with pleasure. 'Home to stay.'

The screech of a gull could be heard over the whining wind and the relentless smack of the waves hitting the beach.

'You're staying?' He narrowed his eyes. 'For how long?'

'I haven't decided—and if I had I wouldn't be telling *you*! My plans are flexible.'

He considered this. 'And *where* exactly will you be staying, Shelley?'

'At my mother's house, of course. Where else?' She glared at him again. 'Sorry. Have I said something funny?'

He shook his head, still laughing. 'Ironic more than funny.'

'That's a little too subtle for me, Drew. Care to let me in on the joke?'

He shrugged, and Shelley's eyes were irresistibly drawn to the hard, strong body moving beneath the thick knit. 'Just that I can't imagine your rich lover gearing up for a night of passion in your mother's old house. Apart from the limitations imposed by the room sizes—the walls are paper-thin!'

'That's not only coarse, it's also inaccurate. Marco has never been a snob!'

'No? Well, then it must be you who has the image problem, mustn't it, Shelley? Because you never brought him back to Milmouth, did you? Not once!' he accused. 'Not even—' and he drew a deep breath '—to your mother's funeral!'

Should she tell him that it hadn't seemed right to do so? That her mother had hated Marco nearly as much as she had adored Drew? It would have seemed disrespectful to her mother's memory to bring along the man she had never stopped blaming for the disintegration of her dreams.

For in Veronica Turner's mind Shelley and Drew would still have been engaged if Marco had not happened along. For a long time Shelley would have agreed with her, but now she recognised that Marco had probably done her a big favour.

Shelley herself had been sick with grief and regret. In fact she had barely been able to function. But apparently that was the normal reaction to sudden death. It had seemed the easier option to handle things on her own. To avoid situations which might create ugly scenes...

'Oh, what's the point in trying to explain?' she questioned tiredly. 'You'll only believe what you want to believe. And I know how much you hate me, Drew.'

'Hate you?' He looked at first surprised and then very slightly perplexed, as if she were being hysterical. 'Hating you would imply that you have some significance in my life, Shelley. And you don't. None at all. Not any more. *Duke!*' The dog came loping over. 'Come on, time to go.'

And he strode off without a word, or even a glance of farewell. Just like that.

She watched him walking away from her across the pebbles and a great tidal wave of sadness rocked her, overwhelming her with its force. Because she had lost everything that once existed between her and Drew, and that was the brutal reality.

The water on the western side of the shore was a deeper shade of blue than the washed-out sky and in his navy sweater and faded jeans Drew seemed to blur and blend into the landscape itself. Shelley watched him and felt a sudden wrench as she remembered the way he had been able to make her laugh.

Remembered the way he had always looked at her—as though someone had just given him a wonderful present. Compare that, she thought, as she swallowed back the memories, with the icy disapproval she had seen on his face just now.

They had been *friends*, she realised—really good friends. And she had thrown it all away. With one irrevocable gesture she had sacrificed that friendship and everything that went with it.

She had made her choices willingly—no one had held a gun to her head. But the reality of what those choices had done to her life invaded Shelley's memory like a dark, stormy cloud.

CHAPTER THREE

SHELLEY had known Drew Glover for as long as she remembered, and she must have known him before that as well.

They had grown up next door to each other in the small, boxy houses which were clustered on the poorer side of Milmouth—a million light years away from the imposing Edwardian villas which overlooked the sea on the western side of the village. She was almost eight years younger than him, and the same age as his youngest sister, Jennie.

Shelley had been brought to Milmouth as a baby, an unsettled, grizzly child whose nature had been forged by uncertainty and insecurity. According to her mother, Drew would bend and pick up the toys she hurled out of her pram and solemnly hand them back to her. But then he had two younger sisters of his own.

'He was such a sweet-natured boy,' Veronica Turner had told her daughter with a beaming smile, the day Shelley and Drew decided to get married. 'And he still is.'

Shelley remembered his curiosity. His protectiveness. He had been the first person who had ever stood up for her—when he overheard one of the other children taunting her.

'So why haven't you got a father, Shelley Turner?'

She had been about seven at the time, an age when she'd desperately wanted to be like everyone else. And

Milmouth was so small and provincial. Everyone else had two parents.

Her face had started working and her mouth had wobbled and she didn't know what she would have answered when Drew had appeared from out of nowhere—tall and tough and teenaged—and had announced scornfully, 'Of *course* she's got a father! Everyone's got a father—hers just doesn't live with her, that's all.'

'Where does he live, then?' one of the others had been bold enough to ask.

Even now Shelley remembered looking into Drew's eyes—so deep and blue and encouraging—and knowing that she should never be ashamed of the truth. If only she had remembered that…'He lives in America,' she'd told the child steadily. 'He's a dentist.'

These two impressive facts had kept the other children quiet for a while, but Shelley had remained an outsider. Veronica Turner had taught her daughter to keep her head down and not make waves. Not to invite people back to the house unless she was really certain that she liked them, and, more importantly, that they liked her. It was better to be considered cold than to risk rejection.

But then, Shelley's mother had known all about rejection. It was a force that had shaped her whole life—a dark, shameful secret she'd kept hidden away. Only Drew knew the full story and Shelley still remembered the day she had told him.

She had been counting cars, sitting on a low wall which separated their little group of houses from the big main road which brought all the holiday-makers into Milmouth during the summer months.

A red car had whizzed by and Shelley had stuck her tongue out between her lips and wrote it down in her notebook.

Drew had been on his way home from the boatyard, where he worked after school, drinking from a can of cola. He'd peered over her shoulder as he passed, then paused.

'What are you doing?'

Shelley shrugged. 'Counting cars.'

He grinned. 'Oh? Make a habit of that, do you?'

'It's for my maths,' she explained. 'Averages and probability.'

He pulled a face and came to perch beside her. 'Who's winning?'

'Blue,' she said. 'I've counted eleven, so far.'

'Oh.' He offered her the can. 'Fancy a slug?'

Shelley shook her head. Money was tight in the Turner household. Never take what you can't repay—her mother had drummed that in to her time and time again. 'No, thanks.'

He stared at her serious little profile. 'Why do you never see your father?' he asked suddenly.

Shelley shrugged. If it had been anyone other than Drew who had asked it, she might have told them to mind their own business. But Drew was Drew.

'I saw him once,' she explained. 'When I was a baby.'

'Just the once?'

'That's right. I was three weeks old.'

'And didn't he want to see you again?'

Shelley blinked furiously as she ticked off another black car in her column. 'That's seven black,' she gulped.

'I'm sorry,' he said instantly. 'I didn't mean to pry.'

She shook her head. 'It's all right for you!' she said, her voice wobbling. 'You've got a mother *and* a father, *and* two sisters!'

He laughed cynically. 'Oh, yeah—it's all right for me! When there are five of us crammed into a house you can't swing a cat in. And my parents are always arguing. So are my sisters! I'll tell you something, Shelley—sometimes I just want to smash my way out of there and never come back!' His blue gaze was piercing. 'Do you really think that everyone's life is so perfect except your own?'

Shelley shook her head in amazement. Drew felt like *that* inside? 'Of course I don't!'

'I won't ask you about your father again,' he told her gently. 'It isn't important.'

But it was important. He had taken her into his confidence and she *wanted* to tell him. Secrets could become unbearable burdens if you didn't share them.

'My father was…*is* a dentist. My mother used to work for him—she was his nurse. They had, like, a big romance. Well, my mum thought it was a big romance,' Shelley shrugged. 'She'd come down from Scotland and she didn't know very much about men.'

Drew nodded thoughtfully, but he didn't say anything.

'Then she found out she was pregnant with me, so she told him…she told him…and he got really mad with her. Said that it had all been a big mistake. And that there was no point in her trying to trap him into marriage—because he already had a wife and children, and they were his "real" children—'

Drew scowled. 'And your mother didn't know that?'

Shelley rounded on him. 'Of course she didn't know that! If she had done she would never have got involved with him in the first place! What sort of woman do you think she is?'

'I didn't mean to insult your mother, Shelley,' he told her, with dignity. 'It just makes me mad when men treat women that way.' He brushed dark, untidy hair back from his face. 'So what happened?'

'Oh, he went back to America with his wife and

''real'' children and Mum brought me here to live. That was the last she ever saw of him.'

'And why Milmouth?' he asked, with interest.

She was grateful for the fact that her instinct had been correct—that Drew wasn't judging her or her mother and finding them wanting.

'She wanted somewhere cheap to live, and couldn't face going back to Scotland with a baby and no father. And she loves the sea.'

He smiled. 'So do I, as a matter of fact. I never want to be away from the sea.'

'Me neither,' she said shyly, smiling back, realising that she had found her true-life hero.

But after that she rarely saw him—their lives diverged and the age-gap was all wrong. Seven years could seem like a generation gap. She knew that he had done well in his school exams, and knew that his teachers had been disappointed when he became an apprentice carpenter. Everyone thought that he'd go away to college.

'It's because he's good at making things,' his mother explained to Shelley on the way back from the shops one day. 'Good with his hands. And he likes the open air—says he doesn't want to be cooped up inside in an office all day. Good luck to him, I say!'

Shelley saw him on the day he left school, with the best grades of his year, and it took every bit of courage she possessed to go up to him and congratulate him. 'I hear you're going to be a carpenter?'

He narrowed his blue eyes at her assessingly. 'What's the matter, Shelley—don't you think I'm aiming high enough?'

She shrugged her shoulders awkwardly. She was only eleven—so what did she know? 'It's not that,' she lied.

'Isn't it?'

'No. I just thought that you'd be—'

'A pilot?' he grinned. 'Or a doctor?'

'Maybe.'

'It's an insecure world, kitten—and people always need houses.'

'I guess they do.' And she blushed with pleasure to hear him call her 'kitten'.

Sometimes, when Shelley was up in her bedroom reading, she used to glimpse him wandering home, stripped to the waist, all honed muscle and bronzed perfection. And the words used to dance like hieroglyphics on the page in front of her.

She was seventeen when he went travelling, originally for a year, but the wanderlust caught him and he was gone for much longer.

She remembered one of the last times she had seen him before he'd left. She'd gone sunbathing further up the bay with a couple of schoolfriends—hidden, they thought, by a large screen of rocks. Feeling liberated and daring, they had removed their bikini tops. But Drew had been out running along the beach, and had seen them. He had gone absolutely ballistic, with Shelley in particular, and her friends had teased her afterwards and said that must mean that he fancied her. And she'd told them that of course he didn't fancy her, because he had barely spoken to her again after that.

And suddenly he had gone.

Shelley had missed him. Missed him like mad. Sometimes she used to go out with his sister Jennie, on Saturday nights. They would go to the Smugglers pub or occasionally to one of the dances at the village hall, or get the bus into Southchester. She'd look at every man and find him wanting, by simple virtue of the fact that he wasn't Drew.

'Has your brother mentioned anything about coming home?' she asked Jennie casually one evening.

Jennie grinned. She was used to women asking her questions about her handsome big brother.

'Nope. Shall I write and say you were asking?'

'Just you *dare*!'

He came back three years later, just before Christmas—when the fairy lights in the pubs twinkled like rainbow drops, reminding him of everything he had missed about England.

Shelley was on her way home from her job as receptionist in Milmouth's upmarket car showroom when she saw him, and had to bite back her pleasure, because she didn't want to gush all over him like a silly little girl.

'Hello, Drew,' she said softly. 'Jennie said you were coming home.'

'Is that really you, Shelley Turner?' he enquired, almost groaning when he realised that this tousled-haired stunner from next door was even *more* gorgeous than when he'd left. He hadn't thought that was possible. But some time in the last three years she had developed the kind of figure that drove men to sin, and her hair was a glossy sheet—the colour of caramel. And he'd forgotten how delicate her skin was and how pale the aquamarine of her eyes.

'Of course it's me!' she giggled. 'Who else did you think it was?'

'I'm not sure,' he answered slowly, his blue eyes looking dazzling in his tanned face. 'Are you going out tonight?'

'Just try and stop me! It's my birthday tomorrow,' she confided. 'And a whole gang of us are meeting up in the Smugglers.'

'Your birthday?' He frowned as alarm bells rang loudly in his brain. 'How old are you?'

She was slightly disappointed that he couldn't remember, but clever enough not to show it. 'I'll be twenty.'

'Wow! You'll be twenty? Well, isn't that just dandy!' His grin showed his relief. 'Mind if I join you?'

Mind? She would have spent all her birthday money on a red carpet if it hadn't looked so obvious! 'No, I don't mind at all,' she answered coolly.

He gave her a boab nut he'd picked up on his travels, with a piece of glittery tinsel tied round it, and sat beside her in the pub, and Shelley didn't want to talk to anyone else but him.

'So did you miss me, little girl?' he quizzed.

She had not yet learnt guile. 'Yes.' But something told her not to let him know how much. 'And I'm a big girl now.'

'So I see.' A pulse began to work in his temple. 'So I see.' To her surprise, he trailed a finger along her cheek and gently tucked a stray strand of hair behind her ear, then frowned. 'Since when did you start wearing mascara?'

She blinked at him, perplexed. 'But I'm not.'

'You mean your lashes have always been that long?' he teased. 'And that dark?'

She laughed. 'I think so! Have you only just noticed, Drew?'

'Mmm. Right this very moment.' He looked terribly thoughtful, and suddenly leaned across and kissed her softly on the lips, in front of the whole pub—and that was that. They became an overnight item. Drew and Shelley. Shelley and Drew. As inseparable as eggs and bacon or peaches and cream.

Drew worked hard for his money. He took a regular job at the boatyard and any other job which came his way—and plenty did. Craftsmen of his calibre were rare enough but coupled with youthful vigour and dedication—well, it seemed that everyone wanted a piece of him. Once a week he went on day release to college and night-times he studied for higher certificates in construction and building.

And the only person who seemed to be missing out was his girlfriend...

'Oh, Drew!' Shelley sighed, one day, when he'd snatched a moment to eat his lunchtime sandwiches with her, sitting side by side on the sea wall. 'You're *always* working!'

'Listen, kitten, the money's good and it's money we need if we want any kind of future together.'

'But I never *see* you any more!'

'You'll see as much of me as you like once we have a place of our own,' he promised, and kissed the tips of her fingers, one by one. 'And guess what?'

'What?'

'The coastguard's cottage is still on the market!' He could barely contain his excitement.

'What, that old place?' Shelley elongated her mouth into a grimace. 'I'm not surprised! They probably can't *give* it away. You'd need to virtually knock it down and start again to make it habitable!'

'But I can do that,' he shrugged modestly. 'That's what I'm training for. That and making you happy.'

'You do,' she pouted, so that he would kiss her.

And when he'd kissed her so that she could barely catch her breath he grinned and said, 'Want to get married?'

'Oh, yes, please!'

'Soon?'

'How soon?'

'Very soon!' he groaned.

He even asked her mother's permission, and Shelley couldn't ever remember seeing her mother look so happy and relieved. Glad that Shelley would have the emotional security she had always longed for.

He bought her a tiny diamond ring which twinkled discreetly on her finger when she held it up to the light.

'It's very *small*,' someone remarked nastily.

'No, it's perfect,' she disagreed fiercely. 'And you're just jealous!'

They decided that they would get married just as soon as they had saved up enough money to buy the coast-guard's cottage and everything was nearly perfect.

But they never made love. Not all the way.

Behind the wooden huts on the windswept beach, their kisses grew wilder, their caresses more frantic—but Drew always calmed things down, made them stop. Shelley felt churned up and bewildered.

She knew that there had been women on his travels. Nothing he'd said, but little things he'd let slip. Sometimes a letter would arrive from some far-off destination and he would scour the envelope and toss it into the bin unread. Once, she saw a postcard from a woman called Angie, the contents of which were graphic enough to make her feel sick.

'And who the hell is Angie?' she demanded.

'She was just a girl I knew,' he answered quietly, ripping the card into tiny little pieces and tossing them into the bin.

She felt sick with jealousy at the thought of what he might have done with Angie and others like her, and she couldn't understand his reluctance to do the same with her.

'You're different,' he told her softly.

She was still smarting over Angie's postcard. 'You'll have to come up with something better than that!'

'Okay. Let me put it this way, then. I don't want you to get pregnant before we're married. It would totally freak your mother out. Shelley, she made me promise to take care of you—and I gave her my word that I would.'

'There are such things as precautions, Drew. We both know that.'

'And they all have risks. We both know that, too. And I want to do things properly with you. You're different,' he said again. 'I love you. I want to spend the rest of my life with you. And the best things in life are always worth waiting for. Trust me.'

But they argued and Shelley ended up feeling headachy and out of sorts and the very next day Marco walked into the showroom to buy a car. He had come all the way from Italy looking for a certain model, and they just happened to have the model he wanted in Milmouth...

Shelley was sitting at her desk, listlessly sorting out some paperwork, when he walked in, looking as if he should be auditioning for the romantic lead in an art film with subtitles.

His physical impact was outstanding—she couldn't deny that, not even to herself. That luminous skin, that crisp black hair. His dark eyes flicked over her casually, like a man used to looking at women. And women not minding a bit.

'Well, hel-*lo*,' he murmured.

She was furious with her heart for beating so fast—furious with herself for reacting. She was an engaged woman—she wasn't *supposed* to find other men attractive. She put on her most repressive expression. 'Can I help you?' she asked him primly.

'Well, that rather depends, doesn't it?' He smiled appreciatively and Shelley was dazzled, flattered. She blushed and his smile curved.

She had never met anyone like him in her life. There was something frighteningly potent about his lazy Latin allure. His was an instinctive sensuality, sweet and seductive as sugar. He was the apple in her Garden of Eden.

He pointed to a long, low silver model—the most expensive in the showroom. 'Will you take me for a drive in that, *cara*?'

'Me?' Shelley shook her head. 'Oh, no—I can't do that. I'll have to get Geoff for you. I'm afraid I don't drive.'

'Oh, yes, you do.' He smiled again. 'You must drive men crazy all the time—with those aquamarine eyes, set in skin the colour of alabaster.'

She couldn't help blushing again at the outrageous compliment. Afterwards she wondered why he had been attracted enough to flirt with her. Her hair had been scraped back into a simple chignon and she wasn't wearing a scrap of make-up. Later still she realised that it had been her innocence which had ensnared him, just as it had ensnared Drew.

Unusually, he persuaded Geoff to *let* him take Shelley for a drive in the car, but then Shelley thought that he probably could have persuaded the tide to turn back, if he'd wanted it to. He was an art dealer—he had his own gallery in Milan. He used extravagant words to describe the paintings he bought and Shelley was fascinated. He told her she was as pretty as a picture, and he would give her a job any time she wanted one.

He bought the car—in cash—to Geoff's delight, and

the following day sent flowers to thank her for her help. A subtle, fragrant mass of sweet peas, and she guiltily buried her nose in the bunched pink and mauve blooms and breathed in their scent. But she left the flowers on her office desk—she didn't dare take them home in case her mother quizzed her about them—and by the next day they had wilted.

She was edgy. Drew had been working so hard that she had hardly seen him. She was getting on for twenty-one and life seemed to stretch out in front of her like a flat, straight road. So when Marco casually offered to take her for a drink after work she found herself wavering. 'I'm not sure.'

'You have a boyfriend?'

She held her left hand up. 'Fiancé,' she said pointedly.

'Maybe I should ask his permission?'

'Oh, no—don't do that!' said Shelley hastily.

He shrugged his shoulders. 'I'm going back to Italy next week,' he explained. 'Maybe I'll call you next time I'm over. Can you get up to London easily?'

It would be easier to get to Mars! She would never see him again. And he was exciting, different, *Italian*. Drew had travelled the world and met lots of interesting people like Marco. What, then—what harm could come of a simple drink?

She had never drunk in the Westward Hotel before. It was on the other side of the village and only the richer tourists could afford to go there, even though the splendour of the place was gradually becoming faded with time.

He led her to a table with a breathtaking view of the sea, and the smell of old leather and the dazzling views and the iced champagne went to her head and made her dizzy.

When Marco drove her home, he stopped a little way from her house and it was like watching a film of someone else's life when he leaned over to kiss her. Shelley told herself it was nothing more than curiosity which made her open her lips beneath his. She'd only ever been kissed by Drew before.

But the kiss was like chocolate; she couldn't stop at one. And it took every bit of will-power she possessed to tear herself out of his arms and run towards the house—with the sound of Fletcher barking madly in her ears and guilt staining her cheeks.

And she hadn't seen the dark figure who stood watching from the shadows of the trees…

The memories dissolved like a dream, and Shelley glanced down at her watch to see that she had been standing gazing at the empty beach for almost an hour. So did that mean Drew really *had* been here, or had she dreamed that up, too?

Slowly she made her way back along the sea-road to where she had left her car, feeling as flat as last night's champagne.

It was ironic, really. She had been thinking how much she had changed and matured. But if that were the case, then how could she so badly have underestimated the impact of seeing him again?

Had she thought she would be immune to him after all this time? Or—worse—imagined that he would pull her into his arms and tell her that he'd never forgotten her?

She slid into the driver's seat and started up the engine.

Time to go home.

CHAPTER FOUR

SHELLEY'S old house looked smaller than she remembered. And scruffier. Paint was peeling from the window panes and the windows themselves were so grubby that they looked like a 'before' shot on a detergent commercial. But the small lawn at the front of the house had been kept clipped and tidy, the borders all neat and weeded. Now who had been responsible for *that*? she wondered as she unloaded the small box of groceries from the car.

She let herself into the house, having to push the door hard to get it open past the small heap of yellowing circulars which had piled up. She shivered. It was cold— bitterly cold—with the smell of damp and disuse penetrating her nostrils with a dank, chilly odour.

She went through the hall and into the tiny sitting room, where the floral wallpaper was beginning to peel in parts, and looked around, nostalgia creeping into her soul like an old friend. On almost every surface stood a photograph—all of Shelley in various stages of growing up.

There she was as a chubby baby, peering out from beneath a cotton bonnet in her pram. There as a toddler on the beach, sucking her thumb and screwing her eyes up at the camera. Another showed her in a too big uniform, self-conscious and proud on her first day at school. And there—a shot of her as an adolescent—leggy and gawky—a child on the brink of womanhood.

But the photo she stared at longest showed her with

Drew. It must have been taken around the time they'd
become engaged—because there was no pretence or coy-
ness about the way they really felt for one another. His
arm was placed lightly around her shoulders but they
weren't looking at the camera—just staring into each
other's faces—giggling with happiness.

Biting her lip, she turned and abruptly left the room,
and went upstairs to her old bedroom.

Nothing had changed there, either. Not a single thing.
The frilly white cover dotted with pink rosebuds still lay
flounced on the small, single bed. The boab nut that Drew
had bought her still sat on the sill of the window where
she used to watch him walk home from work. She had
even kept the piece of tinsel he had tied around it, though
it didn't glitter as brightly any more.

She looked down at the small back garden which had
been her mother's pride and joy, and blinked in aston-
ishment. Because, just like the front, it had obviously
been well looked after, its tidiness contrasting with the
general neglect inside the house.

Carefully clipped herb bushes lined the gravel path and
two bay trees stood in white boxes on either side of the
back door. While at the end, contrasting beautifully
against the dark wooden fence, stood the misty mauve
blur of Michaelmas daisies. For a moment it was like
being transported back in time. Shelley swallowed and
tore her over-bright eyes away—thinking that she might
faint if she didn't have a cup of tea soon.

She went into the kitchen, noting how old-fashioned
the free-standing units looked, and how dingy the paint
was. How dingy everything was, really—when she compared it to the homes she had shared with Marco. Then
she turned the tap on.

Nothing.

Shelley blinked at it in consternation. Then tried the tap again.

Still nothing.

Horror at her own stupidity flared up inside her as she clicked on the light switch, knowing even as she did it that it would prove useless.

She stood there in silence, not noticing the dark shape which had loomed up outside the plastic insert of the front door until a loud rapping made her start.

The sheer height of the man registered on her subconscious as she pulled the door open. But that didn't stop her heart from beating like crazy when she saw it was Drew—still in navy sweater and jeans, but with no sign of the dog.

She looked into his face. It wasn't a friendly face, but it was a face she knew and had once loved. And when you were feeling as vulnerable as Shelley was, feeling that familiarity was a potent and dangerous quality.

'Hello, Drew,' she gulped. 'I certainly wasn't expecting you to be my first caller.'

His mouth flattened into a grim sort of smile. 'Believe me, I wasn't planning on being your first visitor.'

'So why are you here?'

'Curiosity, mainly,' he answered slowly. 'And a phone call from my sister. She insisted I come.'

'Which sister?'

'Jennie.'

'Oh.' Shelley wondered if the regret showed in her face. Because she and Jennie had been the best friends in the world. Until the Marco incident—when, naturally enough, she had taken her brother's side. They hadn't seen one another or spoken a word since. 'How did she know I was here?'

'She's your neighbour. She lives in our old house. And that's next door, in case you've forgotten.'

'Jennie lives *next door*?'

Was this the same Jennie who had called Milmouth a fading seaside dump with no soul? Who had called their small houses rabbit hutches and couldn't wait to get as far away as possible? Shelley's eyes widened with surprise. 'You mean, with your parents?'

'No, no.' He shook his head impatiently. 'They retired to the Isle of Wight. And Cathy's living in London.'

'So how's Jennie?' she dared ask.

'Well, probably more pleased than I am that you've come crawling back—'

'No, not crawling, Drew. With my head held very high.'

'If you say so.' But his eyes glittered as though he didn't quite believe her.

She took a deep breath. 'Drew?'

He threw her a mocking look. 'Shelley?'

'Do you know who has been responsible for doing the garden?'

There was a pause. 'My sister.'

'Your *sister*?' Shelley frowned. 'Jennie must have changed quite a bit if she's into gardening.'

He laughed. 'She doesn't do it herself. She gets someone in for a few hours a week and asked them to keep yours tidy at the same time.' He turned the corners of his mouth down. 'Otherwise it made the place look overgrown and derelict.'

'It looks gorgeous,' she said wistfully.

He didn't respond to that, just fixed her with that dazzling blue stare. 'So where's lover-boy?'

'I do wish you wouldn't keep calling him names!' she told him crossly, then sighed. There was no point in lying. Not to Drew. You only made that kind of mistake once in a lifetime. 'He isn't here.'

'I know. Do you really think I would have come around if he was lurking around upstairs waiting for you?'

'How could you possibly know that?'

'My sister said there was only one person in the car.'

'So Jennie couldn't wait to bad-mouth my arrival?'

He shook his head. 'Actually, no. She saw your car— only she didn't realise that it was your car—and rang me, just in case—'

'In case of what?' Shelley interrupted angrily. 'In case someone in a car happened to be visiting a house? Gosh, I'd forgotten all about how effective the Milmouth mafia could be!'

This seemed to amuse him. 'It depends on how you look at it, surely? Either you find it a repressive, small-town mentality—in which case I wonder why you came back at all—or you appreciate the fact that someone is there looking out for you. If you were a woman, living on her own...as Jennie is...' he paused thoughtfully '...and a car you didn't recognise stopped outside a house which had been empty for the last two years—then you'd be pretty dumb not to investigate, wouldn't you? Particularly if—' and his eyes narrowed with something very like distaste as he half turned his head in the direction of the gleaming grey car which stood outside '—the car in question looked glaringly out of place.'

'And what's wrong with the car?'

'Nothing's wrong with it,' he shrugged. 'It's just a bit of a cliché, isn't it?'

She knitted her carefully plucked brows at him. 'You're calling one of the most aerodynamically superior vehicles in the world a cliché?'

'It's nothing but an executive toy,' he said damningly. 'It reeks of flash and cash, but without much substance. So what was it, Shelley? The pay-off?'

The most galling thing was that he had shrewdly hit on a nerve. 'Mind your own business!'

'Is it all over between you?' he persisted softly. 'Why isn't he here with you?'

Well, she supposed that it was going to come out sooner or later. 'He isn't here because, yes, it's over.'

'You won't be going back?'

'No.' The word fell heavily, like a stone into a pond.

'So what happened?'

She looked at him in surprise. 'I don't have to answer that.'

'No, you're right.' His eyes glittered. 'You don't. But you might want to answer this—which is whether you were intending to come back to a house that hadn't been aired for years, with no running water or electricity. You can't have a bath. You can't flush the loo. You can't even heat yourself a can of soup.' He gave her a look of cool mockery. 'That wasn't very clever of you, was it, Shelley?'

'I left Italy in a…hurry.'

'So I see.' His eyes flicked over the crumpled linen suit. 'Kicked you out, did he?'

She turned away, but not before he had seen the tears well up in her eyes. Tears of fatigue which made her feel like some sad, foolish little cast-off. She swallowed them down. 'Why are you here, Drew—just to insult me? To rile me? Because I can do without it at the moment, if you don't mind.'

'I'll tell you exactly why I'm here,' he told her quietly. 'Because not only is it Sunday, it is also late October. Now, you may have pushed all memories of Milmouth away during your three-year absence, so allow me to re-mind you that the weather isn't particularly welcoming by the sea at this time of year. There's no way you can stay here tonight. You'll freeze. And you won't get water and electricity connected until tomorrow at the very earliest.'

His cool logic made her want to scream at him—mainly because he was right. 'If you're expecting me to fall to my knees in front of you and beg you for help then I'm sorry to disappoint you.'

His eyebrows disappeared into the honey-tipped hair. 'Fall to your knees in front of me any time you like, kitten,' he said deliberately. 'You don't even have to beg!'

Her cheeks flared at the sexual insinuation, but she still managed to meet his gaze with defiance. 'I'll find myself a hotel room for the night!'

'Have you booked?'

'Oh, yeah, sure!' she smiled sarcastically. 'I just came here first to go through the whole pantomime of *pretending* to turn the lights and the water on, while all the time I knew that I had a lovely, warm hotel room waiting for me!'

'You sarcastic little bitch,' he whispered softly. 'I don't know why I came over here with some outdated idea of responsibility. Maybe I should just leave you here on your own.'

'Well, why don't you?' she challenged.

'Because, Shelley—unlike your previous lover—I happen to have a few values, that's why! And not only would I steer clear of muscling in on another man's fiancé—I'd kind of have a problem sleeping easily if I knew that a woman was spending the night alone in a cold and inhospitable house. Even if that woman was you.'

Ouch! 'Don't tell me—you're offering me a bed for the night?'

At her words he stilled, and his eyes glittered with dazzling blue light. *'Oh,'* he murmured. 'Is that what you'd like, then, Shelley? A little body warmth, huh? A little skin on skin? Maybe create a little *friction* together—though I wasn't thinking of the boy scout version of rubbing sticks together—'

'You've been reading too many pornographic magazines!' she suggested tartly.

'I don't think so,' he murmured, his eyes flickering over her in a way which appalled her. 'I never got my kicks that way, kitten.'

'Don't look at me like that, Drew. I don't like it.'

'Liar!' he taunted softly. 'You love it.'

'No, I don't!' But to her dismay her body seemed to agree with him. There was something irresistible about that ruthlessly sexual evaluation and her thoughts began to react to the hunger in his eyes. She tried to push them away, but the images which were being created in her mind were making her head pound and her pulses rocket.

And worse. Her breasts had begun to prickle and swell so that the acutely sensitive tips stung uncomfortably against the crisp lace of her bra. She shifted her weight, hoping that he hadn't noticed.

'No?' He raised his eyebrows and the knowing glint in his eyes told her that he *had* noticed. 'Oh, come, come, Shelley—let's not play the hypocritical little prude! This is me you're talking to, remember? I'm the guy who watched you making out in a total stranger's car. Remember *that*?' He shook his head from side to side. 'If only I'd known you were *that* desperate to have sex, kitten—then I would have happily obliged myself.'

She flinched. 'How many times do I have to tell you that I wasn't "making out"? You know I wasn't!'

'Not technically, perhaps,' he told her coldly. 'If you mean that penetration hadn't actually taken place at that point—'

'Stop it!' she howled, clapping her hands over her ears. 'And please don't be so coarse! I don't have to stand here and listen to—'

'The truth?' he interrupted stonily. 'That's what incenses you so much, Shelley—because it is the truth, isn't it?'

'The truth is far more complex than you make out, Drew Glover! As for your offer of a bed—well, if you think I'm spending the night anywhere near *you*, then you're highly mistaken!'

'I don't remember offering to spend the night anywhere near you. All I asked was whether you'd booked yourself a room.'

'No, I haven't booked,' she said shortly. 'Like I said, I left in a hurry.'

'It's the end of the season,' he reminded her. 'And the only place you stand a chance of getting a room now is at the Westward. But you'll be lucky if you do.'

'The Westward?' Shelley thought of the faded grandeur of the Westward. It cost an arm and a leg and a little more besides to stay there. And whilst she had saved most of her salary during her time in Italy she hadn't planned to register at luxurious hotels which would greedily eat into her capital.

'I expect you'd love to go back there, wouldn't you?' he taunted softly. 'It'll bring all kinds of happy memories flooding back! After all, isn't that where you had your date with the Italian?' He clapped the palm of his hand against his forehead in mock-chastisement. 'Oh, no—I forgot! It was just the one drink, wasn't it? Such a cheap date, aren't you, Shelley?'

It was the last straw. 'I've had about as much as I can take from you, Drew Glover!' She lifted her hand and aimed it at his cheek, but he actually had time to shake his head, before instinctively ducking to avoid it.

'Temper, temper!' he reprimanded softly. 'Though I do like a woman who plays rough! Not a side of our relationship which we ever explored properly, is it, Shelley? More's the pity.'

'*Oh!*' She unballed her fist to produce pink-painted talons as she scrabbled her fingers blindly and frantically towards him, but he was ready for her again.

'Oh, no, pussy-cat!' he murmured, and caught her hand easily, resting her palm against the rough rub of his cheek, so that the drawn fingers softened automatically, like a kitten unsheathing its claws. The pulse in her wrist began to rocket frantically against the curve of his jaw, and he must have felt it too—for he smiled a predatory kind of smile she had never seen before.

She felt a shiver tingling its way up her spine.

'Still excited?' he mocked.

'Disappointed!' she parried. 'I'd like to hit you!'

But he shook his head. 'No. I don't think you would. I think you'd like to be doing something else with me instead. Something which can be equally physical, and just as violent as lashing out at me. Every pore of your body is screaming out for it, but it wouldn't exactly be *appropriate*, now would it, Shelley? So you've sublimated your desire by attempting to hit me instead.' His voice deepened. 'But what the hell, baby? Why not give in to it? What say we go inside and get down on the floor and just *do* it?'

Perhaps the most terrible thing of all was that his

words—instead of horrifying and shocking her—were filling her with the most powerful sense of desire she had ever experienced. Desire so intense that it incapacitated her, making her honey-moist and aching, gazing at him open-mouthed with surrender. 'Stop it!' she croaked.

'Oh, yes, you're turned on, aren't you, Shelley?' he whispered with soft triumph. '*Very* turned on. Those eyes are so wide and dark now, like a cat's. And see how your cheeks burn up. And look here.' He let his gaze drift down to fix with interest on her breasts. 'Tight little buds thrusting towards her lover's eyes—'

'But you're not my lover, Drew!' she gasped out, her voice a kind of choked denial. 'And you never were!'

'No,' he agreed. 'I'm not. But there's plenty of time to remedy that.'

'Never, never, never!' she chanted. 'So do me a favour and get out!'

'Sure?'

'As sure as—'

'*Drew!* Drew, are you still in there?'

Disorientated and still caught up in the hypnotic throb of desire, Shelley stared at him. 'Who's that?' she whispered.

'My sister,' he said, with a grim smile. And, letting go of Shelley's hand, he pulled open the front door and Shelley found herself face to face with Jennie Glover.

It had been three years since she had last seen Drew's sister, when she had left Milmouth under such a cloud—and Shelley mentally geared herself up for her disapproval.

But, outwardly at least, Jennie appeared to be quite composed—there was none of her brother's lip-curling condemnation. In fact, Drew's sister had changed quite radically and Shelley kept her face completely straight, hoping that her surprise at the other woman's appearance didn't show.

Jennie had shared many of Drew's physical character-istics—they had both been tall with athletic builds, and the shiny hair and clear skin which came from natural good health. But Jennie had changed.

She seemed smaller than Shelley remembered—though maybe that was because her shoulders were hunched up, like a person who constantly doubted herself. Her thick dark hair was unkempt and badly in need of styling, and her skin was sallow and dull. But it was her figure which startled Shelley most. She hadn't just gained weight—she had gained it in the most unlikely of places. She had a real pot for a belly and her slumped posture only em-phasised it. She wore an old pair of jeans and a dirty sweater and looked light years away from the smiley-eyed girl of yesteryear.

Shelley felt a great wave of nostalgia for how things used to be. They had once been friends and seeing her now brought back how much she had missed that close-ness. 'Hello, Jennie,' she said quietly. 'It's good to see you again.'

'Hello, Shelley.' Jennie's face creased into a smile which looked genuine. 'You probably thought that I was an interfering busy-body ringing up Drew and sending him round here—'

'It's okay. I realise that you were just being a good neighbour.' Shelley smiled back. 'It was dumb of me not to have planned my return a little better.' But Marco's bombshell had caught her unawares.

'I was worried about you being without any heating at this time of year,' Jennie explained. 'It's been unbeliev-ably cold here, and I thought that after Italy—' She bit her lip as if she'd put her foot in it. 'Er—it's just that

Drew has had central heating installed in *our* house, but
your mother—God rest her soul—never got round to it.'

Several of Jennie's words lodged themselves stubbornly in Shelley's mind, where they refused to shift. She
frowned with confusion. 'Drew has had central heating
installed?' she repeated, like a child learning tables. She
looked up at him, her face freezing in horror as she imagined having him that close.

'Don't tell me you're still living at home, Drew!' she
exclaimed in surprise. Only as soon as the words were
out of her mouth did she become aware of how prepos-
terous they sounded. As if this vibrant, virile man would
still be living at his parents' old house.

Yet Jennie was…

Drew gave a shout of laughter only slightly less explosive than his sister's. 'Er, no. I'm not, as it happens.'

'Drew?' Jennie snorted, and for the first time her face
came to life as it lit up with amusement. 'Living at
home?' She turned to her brother. 'Can you imagine?'

'Oh, I can imagine it as clearly as Shelley obviously
can,' he drawled, his eyes glinting provocatively in
Shelley's direction. 'It's amazing the places that your
imagination can take you, if you want it to. And we can
all see where Shelley's imagination is taking her! Wish-
fulfilment, I believe it's called. Yeah, I've still got my
old room at home, kitten—and this time there'll be nothing to stop you from visiting me there!'

'I'm sorry,' said Shelley very stiffly. 'I obviously mis-
understood what you meant.' She discovered that another
stupid lump had risen in her throat, and she swallowed
it down like poison. She wondered where he *was* living,
but was damned if she was going to ask. That might look
as though she cared.

'So what are you planning to do now you're here, Shelley?' asked Jennie. 'Are you back for good?'

It was a question which she was damned if she was going to consider under the critical eye of Drew Glover. 'I haven't decided what I'm doing. I'm just going to sit back and take stock for a little while.'

Jennie looked round the hall and shivered. 'Well, it's freezing in here,' she said. 'You can't possibly stay here tonight.'

'I've suggested to Shelley that she stay at the Westward,' Drew put in. 'That's the only place where she'd be likely to get a room at this time of year.' He turned to Shelley, his eyes glinting with devilment. 'And if the car you're driving is anything to go by, then you shouldn't have a problem affording it.'

'A problem?' she snapped. 'I think I can just about afford the Westward's prices!'

Jennie screwed her face up. 'Though I suppose there's no reason why I shouldn't offer to put you up for a couple of nights.'

A look passed between brother and sister. Did Shelley imagine it, or did Drew shake his head very slightly? 'I don't think that's a good idea,' he said softly.

He looked at her in that unhurried and insulting way he seemed to have perfected, his eyes flickering from the tip of her expensive leather boots up to the small diamond which glittered on a platinum chain at her throat and which matched the thin bangle at her wrist. 'I think that Shelley has become too much of a hothouse flower to ever consider staying with you, Jennie!'

Shelley blushed. 'Oh, please! By implying that I'm a snob—which I'm *not*—you have also managed to insult your sister!' She glared at him. 'Besides which, I don't need you to answer for me, Drew!'

Jennie gave a small smile. 'It's not insulting,' she told Shelley. 'Drew's right. It *is* a bit cramped in there.'

Shelley wondered how that could be. Five of them used to live there—and if their parents and Drew and Cathy had all gone then that left two spare bedrooms, according to Shelley's calculations. But now did not seem a good time to ask. And besides, she really *didn't* want to stay with Drew's sister. Jennie would doubtless paint a rosy picture of how wonderful his life had been without her and she didn't think she could face hearing it. Not at the moment.

'I'm sure it isn't cramped,' she said briskly. 'I spent many happy years growing up here and I'm the last person who would ever turn their nose up at a small house. But Drew's right. I wouldn't dream of imposing on you.'

'I'll tell you what, Jennie,' said Drew, in a lazy voice which nonetheless sounded very like a command. 'Why don't you take Shelley home and give her a cup of tea, while I drive on up to the Westward and see if they have a room for her?'

Shelley met his forceful blue stare. 'You don't have to do that for me.'

'I know I don't,' came the silky reply.

'Then why?'

'Like I said,' he drawled, 'I seem to be stuck with this annoying streak of chivalry and at heart I guess I'm just a gentleman. The Westward is full for most of the year now—and I wouldn't want you going up there on a wild-goose chase—not if they don't have a room.'

She looked at him assessingly. 'I'm not sure I believe you.'

'Well, whether you do or whether you don't, the fact remains that you still need a warm bed for the night—'

'There's always the telephone,' murmured Shelley, unwilling to be obligated to him. 'Why don't we ring them and see?'

He shook his head. 'Oh, no!' he argued softly. 'The telephone is never as effective as face-to-face contact—surely you must have learnt *that* by now, Shelley! So why don't you let me go and sweet-talk them into giving you one?'

'Sweet-talk them? And how will *you* do that?' she laughed. 'You've got friends in high places now, have you, Drew?'

Only the merest quirk of his mouth betrayed his irritation. 'Oh, I've done a bit of work for them, off and on over the years. They've always treated their tradesmen well.'

'I'll go and put the kettle on.' Jennie giggled. 'Come next door and have some tea with me, Shelley. You're very welcome.'

Shelley nodded. 'I will. Thank you.'

'Wait for me, Jennie,' Drew murmured, then turned back to Shelley. 'Why don't we leave you to lock up at your own pace? Maybe you still want a little time to get reacquainted with the house, after such a long time away,' he suggested, with such apparent good sense that Shelley felt she had no choice but to agree. She couldn't put her finger on it, but she had the distinct impression she was being manipulated—but quite frankly she was too tired to object.

She stood at the window and watched them go, feeling that her heart might break as he walked with his sister back down the road of their childhood.

CHAPTER FIVE

SHELLEY opened all the bedroom windows and a small one in the bathroom, catching an unexpected glimpse of herself in the hall mirror as she went back downstairs.

She shuddered and halted in her tracks. What a sight she looked!

In the two days since she had been travelling she hadn't given a thought to her appearance, and my—how it showed! If she had thought that Jennie Glover wasn't looking her best, then Drew's sister must have been having similar thoughts about *her*. She looked as if she had been through the mill and back.

Her face was pale and pinched and the short, usually immaculate hair looked far from immaculate—the wind had swept it out of shape and it badly needed the attention of a hairdresser. She squinted at her reflection—at aquamarine eyes which were smudged with mascara, with shadows of fatigue beneath, like dark blue thumbprints. No wonder Drew had been so rude about her appearance.

She found her soap bag and cleansed her face, brushed her teeth and ran her fingers through her hair. When she had finished she felt a bit better. Not much—but it was a start.

What she wanted more than anything else was a long, hot bath and to put her head on a feather-down pillow and sleep for a week. But in the meantime she would settle for a cup of tea with Jennie.

Locking the door behind her, she made her way to the

house next door, and Jennie must have been looking out for her, for she opened the front door before Shelley had a chance to knock. She had run a comb through her hair and applied a coat of pink lipstick and Shelley thought that she looked much better, though there was still that sense of defeat which made her eyes look so hollow.

'Come in,' she said. 'Only excuse the mess!'

Shelley stepped inside the house and the first thing that struck her was how different it felt from the house she remembered.

For a start, it was deliciously warm—like a tropical paradise compared to the icy temperature of her own house—with slim, top-of-the-range radiators shimmering out their heat.

She wriggled her shoulders luxuriously. 'It feels fantastic in here, Jennie—so lovely and warm.' She looked around the hall. 'And it's beautifully decorated, too.'

'Why, thank you! Come into the sitting room—it's even nicer in there,' smiled Jennie. 'And I've made a tray of tea.'

'Lead me to it!' murmured Shelley.

The sitting room was immaculate, with freshly painted walls and an expensive-looking carpet covering the floor. There were two terracotta sofas, with jade-green cushions scattered over them, and, in the centre of the room, a coffee-table on which stood a tray of tea and biscuits.

On the sideboard stood a large, silver-framed portrait of a baby in a white cotton dress, with dark curls of hair fizzing around her face. Was that Cathy's baby? Shelley wondered.

'Sit down,' said Jennie.

'Thanks!' Shelley sank thankfully down onto one of the sofas. 'Though I'm so tired that I wonder whether I'll ever be able to get up again!' She looked around. 'This room is *amazing*, Jennie—it looks twice the size of mine! You must have spent a lot of time or a lot of money doing it up—or both!'

'Oh, that was Drew, not me,' Jennie explained as she poured the milk out. 'I had to go into hospital, and while I was there he arranged for the house to be modernised. Heating, carpets, curtains. The lot. It was such a surprise when I came home!'

Shelley's lips formed a reluctant O. 'Generous of him,' she commented reluctantly.

Jennie frowned. 'He *is* very generous—surely you've noticed that before!'

'Well, of course I have! I was engaged to the man, Jennie—and I got to know his good points pretty well.' Something stirred deep in her subconscious. 'Does he pay for your garden to be done, too?' she asked suddenly.

'Yes, he does.'

'So he's been paying for mine all this time, as well?'

Jennie looked awkward. 'He'd hate you to make a big deal out of it. It was starting to look tatty and he asked the gardener to keep it looking neat, that's all.'

Shelley shook her head. 'No, that's not all. He's done more than that—it looks almost as good as when my mother was alive.' She sighed. If only he didn't have so *many* good points—like that streak of innate thoughtfulness which used to have her mother and her friends eating out of his hands.

'He must be doing well,' she observed slowly. 'To be able to afford to do all this for you. Money was tight when we were together.'

'That's one of the reasons you left him, isn't it?'

Shelley gave her a steady look. 'Is that what you think?'

Jennie shrugged. 'What were we supposed to think?

You left him for a very rich man. A man you didn't really know. So obviously that was the first thing which sprang to mind.'

'Did everyone else think that, too?'

'Pretty much. Shall I pour you some tea?'

'Please.'

Jennie handed over a steaming mug and fixed Shelley with a curious look. 'But now you're back.'

'Yep.' Steam wafted up her nostrils. She waited for the inevitable question.

'Why?'

'That depends who wants to know—you or your brother?'

'I suspect that Drew's need to know is greater than mine,' said Jennie drily. 'But most other people will be curious once they find out you're back. You know what this place can be like.'

Yes, she knew. But despite the cloying drawbacks of a small town she knew something else, too, something which came straight from the heart. 'I've come back because it's my home,' she said quietly. 'It's the first place I thought of.'

Jennie looked at her shrewdly. 'I thought that home was an apartment in Milan and a villa on Lake Garda?'

The details were much too precise to masquerade as casual gossip. 'Who on earth told you that?'

'Drew did. Soon after you'd gone.'

'Drew? I didn't realise he knew. My mother must have told him, I suppose.'

Jennie shrugged. 'Even if she hadn't he would have found out anyway. Like he always says—knowledge is power.'

'Does he?' It sounded more like something *Marco*

would say. 'I never heard him say anything like that before.'

'No, well…' Jennie looked slightly uncomfortable. 'It's been a long time.'

'Yes.' Shelley leaned back and noticed the plastic box full of toys stuffed behind one of the sofas. And the sense of something being different which had struck her as she'd first entered at last began to make sense. 'You've got a child living here, haven't you?'

'Yes, I have. A baby, actually. *My* baby!' Jennie smiled with maternal pride. 'You saw the toys in the box?'

'Yes, I did, and the photo on the bureau. But I noticed something different when I first walked in. The place had that air that all houses with children in them have—of everything being tidied away while the baby's asleep! I could always tell which of Marco's friends had children and which didn't,' she added.

'Didn't he want any children of his own?'

'Not when I was with him,' answered Shelley truthfully.

'I see.' Jennie reached out for a biscuit, then changed her mind. 'I've put on too much weight recently.'

'Well, if you've just had a baby…'

'That's no excuse.'

'I suppose not.' Shelley reached for a biscuit and, meeting Jennie's eyes, shrugged. 'Your brother thinks that I could do with gaining a few pounds.'

'Well, you *are* terribly thin.' Jennie's stare was hard and bright. 'So is Marco off the scene for good?' she asked suddenly.

Shelley laughed, oddly refreshed by her candour. 'That's a bit of a jump from discussing babies and waistlines!'

'Is it? I thought Marco was the love of your life. And if that was the case, didn't you want his baby?'

This question rocked her. Its intimacy jangled at her raw nerves and Shelley was acutely aware that anything she told Jennie would get straight back to Drew. And if she told the truth, wouldn't that damn her even more in their eyes? 'I'd rather not talk about Marco, if you don't mind. Tell me about your baby instead.'

Jennie beamed. 'She's eight months old and the most adorable child on the planet,' she said, getting up and taking a photo album from the sideboard. She handed it to Shelley. 'Although I recognise that I might be a little biased!'

'What's her name?'

'Ellie. Look—that one was taken just after she was born.'

'She's sweet. She's sleeping now, is she?'

Jennie shook her head. 'No. She's out for the day, with her…father.'

Shelley had been flicking through the album, but she glanced up when she heard Jennie's hesitation. 'You don't *have* to tell me, you know.'

'Oh, it's not a big, dark secret and I'm not ashamed of being a single mother,' said Jennie defensively. 'You know him, actually. Or you did. Remember Jamie Butler?'

Shelley nodded as she took another biscuit and bit into it. 'Of course I do. He was ahead of us at school—a few years below Drew—am I right? Always very tanned—loved boats? Blond curly hair? Good-looking?'

'That's the one,' said Jennie wistfully. 'He still loves boats, and Ellie adores him. So do I.'

It wasn't her place to pry. 'That's nice,' said Shelley evenly.

'No, it isn't nice,' disagreed Jennie mulishly. 'It's hell, if you must know.'

'Because you're no longer together, you mean?'

'We never were, not really. Not for long.' Jennie sighed. 'But he wants us to be.'

'And you don't?'

Jennie shook her head. 'Drew doesn't.'

'*Drew?* What the hell does it have to do with Drew?'

Jennie gave a hollow laugh. 'Everything. He's my self-appointed moral guardian, didn't you know?'

'Sounds familiar,' gritted Shelley. 'Drew knows best. Or thinks he does.'

'Exactly,' sighed his sister, briefly forgetting sibling loyalty. 'And basically he disapproves of Jamie because Jamie can't provide for me in the way that Drew thinks he should.'

'You may think this is none of my business—' Shelley took a last mouthful of tea and stood up '—but Drew is the world's biggest control freak—he always has been. And it's your life, not his. We only get one bite at the cherry—so don't let him make you live it in a way which makes you unhappy!'

'If only it were as simple as that!'

'Everything is as simple as you make it,' said Shelley fiercely. 'Believe me. If you want Jamie then you've got to fight for him.' The way she should have fought for Drew. She'd thought that for a long time afterwards until she had realised that those kind of reflections would get her precisely nowhere. She glanced at her watch. 'It's time I was going. If the Westward won't take me—'

'Then come back!' said Jennie impulsively. 'I mean it.'

'I know you do. And thanks. Thanks for the tea, too.'

'But I'll see you again, won't I?' said Jennie. 'Once

your house is habitable enough to move in. You aren't just going to take off somewhere again, are you?'

'Who knows?' said Shelley truthfully. She didn't know how living back in Milmouth would affect her. Seeing Drew some days—maybe most days. Especially if he was involved with someone...

'Does Drew have a girlfriend?' she asked Jennie suddenly, then wished she could have bitten the question back. 'I'm sorry. It isn't fair of me to ask you.'

'No, it isn't,' Jennie agreed. 'Though it's understandable. He doesn't talk about his personal life to me! Though I guess if there was something really serious going on I'd know about it.'

'But I suppose he's been out with other women since I've been away?'

Jennie looked at her in exasperation. 'It's been three years, Shelley—of *course* he has! Why, he still gets mail from some of the women he met when he was travelling—and you know how long ago that was!'

'You won't tell him that I wanted to know? He might take it the wrong way.' Or the right way.

Jennie shook her head. 'I can't promise not to tell him, not if he asks. He's my brother and I love him. And you hurt him, you know.'

'Yes, I know,' said Shelley. 'I'm the one who has to live with what I did.' But in the end she suspected she had hurt herself far more... 'Goodbye, Jennie,' she smiled.

But once outside there was no need to keep up the pretence and the smile fell away as she slid into her car, not switching on the engine until she had composed herself. Then she found herself revving up like a racing driver, until she remembered where she was, and she drove almost sedately up the winding cliff road towards the Westward Hotel.

The late afternoon sun was pale and golden and the tall maritime conifers which lined the coastal road leading to the hotel gave the place a very European flavour.

But Drew's words came back to haunt her as she approached the hotel. This had been where Marco had brought her. Where she, foolish girl that she had been, had sealed her fate—her head turned by expensive wine and extravagant gestures.

Yet she had passively agreed to let Drew book her a room here, without bothering to challenge his assertion that she wouldn't find one anywhere else. Was that simply because she was exhausted from travelling, or because she had always found the force of his character too much to withstand? Maybe he thought that a night at the Westward would unsettle her enough to make her leave as abruptly as she had arrived.

She eased her foot off the accelerator, seriously tempted to go and search out a place advertising bed and breakfast.

But a little B and B was bound to have a curious landlady. Someone who might know her, and her history. At least this place was big enough to provide the privacy and the solitude she craved—if only for tonight, until her turbulent emotions had settled themselves down.

She drove in through the gates of the Westward and parked the car, immediately noticing how the surrounding grounds had been spruced up. The gardens and flowerbeds didn't just look immaculate—they looked as if they'd been lovingly re-created by someone with an instinctive eye for colour and harmony.

The hotel had been built as a private home at the end of the last century and stood overlooking the bay, silhouetted against the intense light which glittered in off the sea. It had always been an impressive building, but its star had been on the wane when Shelley had left.

Now she could see that money and love had clearly been lavished on it since her last visit—for the once crumbling brickwork had been righted, the paintwork replenished, and tired-looking guttering replaced.

It would not have looked out of place in any of the most upmarket European resorts, she decided as she carried her bags into the main hall, where the light spilled rich, royal colours through stained glass onto the polished wood floor.

The woman behind the reception desk looked up and smiled and Shelley was even more taken aback. Even the receptionists seemed to have had a revamp! This one had dark, glossy red hair and the luminous pale skin which sometimes accompanied it—accentuated by the iris-blue suit she was wearing. She looked about the same age as Shelley but there all similarity ended—because her well-groomed serenity couldn't have provided more of a contrast to the crumpled sight that Shelley must have made.

'Can I help you?' she asked pleasantly.

'I'm Shelley Turner,' she answered, wondering why she found herself suddenly feeling ever so slightly intimidated. She was *used* to quiet luxury. She looked around. There was no sign of Drew, and she didn't know whether to be glad or sad. Should she mention him by name? 'Did a man—?' Now how stupid did *that* sound? 'I believe someone may have tried to reserve a room for me?'

'Yes, they did, Miss Turner,' said the woman smoothly, without even bothering to look down at her reservation list. 'You're in the Lilac Suite. Shall I have someone take you straight up there?'

'Suite?' Shelley squeaked. The Westward had gone decidedly upmarket if it was now providing suites! 'I didn't want a suite! Nothing grand—just a room for the night, that's all.'

'I'm afraid that was the only one available.' The woman shrugged apologetically. 'Of course, if there's a problem with that, I can speak to—'

'No, there's no problem.' She was dying to ask for a price list, but didn't dare. She'd stayed in enough plush places with Marco to know that if you had to ask how much something cost, then that implied you couldn't afford it! And, no matter how much it cost to stay at the Westward, she could certainly afford one night.

The woman gave a polite, professional smile. 'Then I'll have someone show you upstairs, shall I, Miss Turner?'

'Yes, please.'

A porter took her bags and led the way up the curving staircase and right along to the end of a portrait-strewn corridor, where he flung open a pair of double doors. Shelley peered over his shoulder and became aware of a room which was softly glowing in pale shades of pinkish-violet. Slinky, sensuous and decadently sumptuous. She blinked.

This? In *Milmouth*?

'The Lilac Suite, miss.'

She fumbled around for a tip.

'That's very kind of you, miss. Will you be wanting anything else?'

'Not at the moment, thanks. What time is dinner?'

'We start serving at seven-thirty, miss.' He closed the door quietly behind him.

Once he'd gone she looked around properly. It was the most amazing room she had ever seen—and she was no stranger to amazing rooms. Acres of mauve carpet, as soft and rich as velvet, while the vast four-poster bed was partially concealed by heavy and lavish hangings in lilac picked out with gold. The colour scheme was echoed by the silky curtains which were draped in shimmering lilac columns at either side of the floor-to-ceiling windows.

And the view...

Shelley walked over to one of the windows and gazed out with pleasure at the uninterrupted view of the English Channel, and it took her breath away. How had she forgotten just how stunning her childhood home could be?

Further exploration revealed that the adjoining bathroom had an old-fashioned claw-footed bath the size of a small swimming pool. Now *that* was what she needed more than anything else!

She turned the taps on, added some essence, and let the water gush in while she undressed, jerkily peeling off the white lacy underwear she had bought in Milan. She tossed it in a filmy heap on the floor, thinking ruefully that she'd better invest in something more substantial now that she was back.

When the bath was almost full, she climbed in and sank beneath the foam, sighing with sheer pleasure as the warm water caressed her skin like silk.

She washed her hair, then lay back, feeling her body begin to relax properly for the first time since Marco had told her that he had fallen in love. Love. Horrible word. What did it mean? It meant disruption, that was what it meant! The perfumed vapour enclosed her and she felt her eyelids grow heavy as sleep—or something very close to sleep—claimed her senses and she gave herself up to it.

She didn't hear the bathroom door slide slowly open or the momentary pause before it was eased shut again, but something must have registered in her subconscious because when she opened her eyes again it was to see Drew standing there, very still, just watching her.

It was too unexpected and much too close to fantasy for her to make any initial reaction other than one of dazed recognition. She sank a little lower into the bath water as she stared up at him. And there was a lot to stare at. In the confined space of the steamy room, his long legs seemed to go on for ever.

The jeans which she had admired on the beach—was that really just a few short hours ago?—looked even better on closer inspection. Soft blue denim brushed against taut thigh, whispered against knee and tapered down to ankle.

Her eyes drifted upwards, to where the simple white T-shirt hugged exactly where it should, caressing the firm, tight flesh of his torso like a lover.

The steam and fatigue had lulled her. The cloudy mist which had moistened the air now clogged her brain with sensation. Sapphire eyes blazed down at her in silent question, and beneath the warm, creamy foam Shelley felt the flowering of desire.

'Drew!' she breathed.

'Hello, Shelley.'

She sank down even deeper, so that the visible swell of her breasts was covered by the little islands of foam which floated on the surface. 'What are you doing here?' she whispered, wondering why she wasn't screaming at him to get out.

'Truthfully? Apart from getting more turned on by the second? I'm just fantasising about what lies beneath all those bubbles.' His mouth tightened. 'And realising that I've never seen you completely naked before. Do you realise that, Shelley? Incredible, isn't it, when you think about it?'

Desire shafted a path from the tips of her breasts over the soft curve of her belly, and beyond, where a moist, slow throb had begun to torment her.

'Drew.' It was meant to be a protest, so why did it come out as some aching little plea?

'I've seen you in a swimsuit many times, of course,' he said, matter-of-factly, with all the passion of someone describing a computer program. 'And once—just once— when you were topless on the beach. Do you remember that, Shelley?'

Of course she remembered. How could she ever forget? But it had been a long time since she had allowed herself to think of it in any detail. She shook her head. 'N-no. I don't think so.'

'Then let me refresh your memory.'

'Drew—'

'You were seventeen.' He cut across her weak objection, his voice low and deliberate. 'And it was the end of that long, baking summer just before I went travelling. Remember that? It was so hot and so still that every breath you took seemed to scorch the lining of your throat. You and a couple of the other girls were sunbathing behind the rocks in that little cove further up the bay. Now do you remember?'

She nodded, her lips too dry to speak, despite the dampness of the steamy air.

He narrowed his eyes, taking in her inertia and her heavy eyelids. 'You'd all stripped down to bikini bottoms. And yours was gold—so that it looked all hard and shiny—yet it clung like syrup to the curve of your hips. And I didn't even notice the others. I couldn't see them. All I could see was you. You. And your skin was glistening, just as it's glistening now. Soft, creamy breasts topped with tight little rosebuds...' He let his voice trail away.

'Drew, please—' she managed, wondering whether he knew that those rosebuds were tightening now beneath the concealing blanket of foam.

'I'd been running and I was pouring with sweat, and I saw you stretched out on a towel with your arms raised so languidly above your head, and I could barely move—' It had been one of the most exquisitely frustrating erections of his life, and in forcing himself to quell it he had only succeeded in making himself ache all the more.

'Drew, don't—' She moved her hips restlessly. 'Don't...'

Ignoring her plea, he simply stared very hard at her. 'And do you remember what I did next?'

'You shouted at me and threw me your T-shirt,' she responded dully. 'And told me to cover myself up.'

'So I did.' He gave a disbelieving laugh as he recalled the hypnotic lure of seeing her pale flesh contrasted against the darker curves of the baking pebbles. That lure had kept him abroad far longer than he had intended, for he'd seen the danger she represented—a danger he had not contemplated at that stage in his young life.

Yet, perversely, the more he denied it, the more her allure had stubbornly refused to go away. And every woman he was intimate with in those subsequent years wore shiny gold bikini bottoms in the fevered longings of his mind.

He came and crouched down beside the bath, so that his face was on a level with hers, and she found that she couldn't look away from the compelling blue blaze of his eyes. 'God—what a fool I was with you, Shelley. To be so in awe of your innocence that I let it control me!'

She shook her head, but it felt weighted and useless, too heavy for her neck. 'Nothing controls you, Drew. You're the one who does the controlling.'

He reached his hand out and trickled a finger down the damp flush of her cheek, feeling the unresisting silk of her skin. 'Am I really?' he questioned softly. 'No, I don't think so. I let my conscience control me for too long— protecting my innocent bride-to-be, when all the time she couldn't wait…couldn't wait for marriage and the man she professed to love. You wanted sex so badly that you were prepared to give yourself to the first man who came along, weren't you, Shelley?'

She leaned her head back against the bath, too weary to protest, too comfortable to move. 'I'm too tired to argue with you,' she sighed. 'It wasn't like that.'

'Oh, yes, it was,' he contradicted forcefully. 'You know damned well it was!'

She shook her head. 'No, Drew. You placed me on an impossible pedestal—which you seemed to glory in smashing from underneath my feet! It was all right for you! You'd lived a little; you'd gone travelling and tasted all that the world had to offer. And then you came home to your virgin bride—how perfect! But you never gave a thought to *my* needs, or *my* feelings, did you? You couldn't resist those women abroad, but you could certainly resist me!'

'So the way you behaved was *my* fault—is that what you're saying, Shelley?'

Suddenly he stood up and moved away and her eyes followed him, missing him, needing him, wishing that she could travel back in time and that everything could be so different.

But it couldn't. And she wasn't going to open herself up to more hurt by hankering after a man who had no interest in her other than sexual. Especially a man who had once loved her.

He stood there staring down at her, his face a weave of complex planes and shadows, and she wondered if he was aware of how much she desired him.

Even after all this time.

'Get out,' she mumbled, her eyelids feeling as if someone had perched lead weights on them.

He frowned. 'I'm not going anywhere until I'm convinced that you're not going to fall asleep. Do you have any idea of how long you've been lying there?'

'Not long enough!' She struggled to keep her eyes open and finally got around to asking what she should have asked the moment he'd nonchalantly strolled into the bathroom. 'What are you doing here, anyway?'

'I thought I'd better check you hadn't drowned.' He looked into her rosy face, at the dilated pupils of her drowsy eyes. She was looking at him as though she *was* drowning, he observed thoughtfully, before closing his mind to that wide-eyed appeal.

'And did you just happen to be passing?' she asked him sleepily. 'Or do you go around playing guardian angel to all the female guests? Barging into their bathrooms and leering at them?'

'No, I make an exception for you, Shelley.' He laughed softly. 'I always did. As for leering—that kind of implies that it's unwanted attention, and I certainly didn't hear you objecting a minute ago! In fact, I rather got the feeling that you were sorry I stopped.'

'Well, you would, wouldn't you? The phrase may have gone out of fashion—but you obviously haven't moved with the times since you are the original male chauvinist pig, Drew Glover!'

'Ah, but pigs can be very lovable animals, Shelley!

Now why don't you let that water out and catch up on some sleep before I buy you dinner?'

She very nearly sat up in indignation, but remembered where she was just in time, and contented herself with a snort instead. 'You have to be out of your tiny little mind!'

'Very probably.'

'You seriously think I want to have dinner with you?'

He shook his head. 'No, that's just the thing—I don't. Certainly not on any sensible, rational level. Any more than I wish to have dinner with you. And yet at the same time there is nothing I want more, and the same goes for you, Shelley. If I go home and eat supper alone—or even with someone else—I'll spend the whole evening thinking about you. Wondering about you. What your life has been and whether it's lived up to all its promise.'

'I'm flattered!'

'Oh, don't be!' His mouth flattened. 'It's only like the scratching of an itch, or the slaking of a thirst. I don't want you to be an enigma any more—so let's have dinner as equals. Simple. An equal I can deal with.'

'Deal with?' she questioned uncertainly.

'Sure. We both know that there is a sense of unfinished business between us, and don't deny it, Shelley, because I can read in your eyes that you agree. It's an interesting but rather annoying dilemma, isn't it? For both of us to be drawn so irresistibly towards something we'd both rather forget? But at least this time my desire for you is not restricted by any outdated morals. So—' he raised his brows '—dinner?'

'What if I told you I'm not hungry?'

'Then I'd be justified in calling you a liar!' he retorted softly, staring down at the highest cheekbones he had ever seen on a woman. 'But telling the truth was never your strong point, was it, Shelley?' He stared down at the pinched paleness of her face. 'You look bloody awful as it is—and I don't want you collapsing on me.'

'Why should *you* care whether I collapse or not, Drew?'

'Care?' He laughed, but it was the emptiest sound she had ever heard. '"Care" wouldn't be my word of choice, Shelley. Let's just say that it's about time we tied up the loose ends left over from our relationship once and for all. Maybe then we'll both be free of whatever it is that still binds us.'

'And for tying loose ends I presume you're talking about sex?'

'Well, I certainly don't mean a restrained courtship,' he answered cruelly. 'Been there; done that!'

'You are a hard, hard man!' she shot back, then wished she could bite her words back as she saw his arrogant responding smile. She waited for some remark which was heavy with innuendo.

But Drew was never predictable.

'Just get out of the tub, Shelley,' he growled as he swung out of the bathroom.

CHAPTER SIX

SHELLEY was covered in goosebumps as she climbed out of the bath once Drew had gone. She dipped her hand in and fished around in the soapy water to find the plug and let it out. The water was now almost completely cold! But her teeth stopped chattering once she had wrapped herself in the monstrous bathrobe which hung on the back of the door. She stood by the open door of the bathroom, put her head to one side, and listened.

Nothing.

Her breathing sounded magnified in her ears as she went back into the lilac bedroom, half expecting to see him arrogantly sprawled out on the shiny expanse of the bed, but the room looked empty.

'Drew?' Her voice sounded indistinct. 'Are you still in here?'

Feeling a little like an amateur detective, she even peeped behind the silky lilac curtains, until she had satisfied herself that he had definitely gone!

Except that satisfied was probably as inappropriate a description for her as 'care' had been for him. She felt far from satisfied—more angry with herself and with him. And mixed up, too—because, yes, she still wanted Drew as much as he clearly wanted her. She had known that from the moment they had seen one another on the beach. Only this time he was not being held back by some old-fashioned sense of what was right. He had told her *that*, too, and with heartbreaking honesty.

So why hadn't he just pounced while she had been

lying naked in the bath, getting turned on to an exquisite pitch by the things he was saying to her? It had been the perfect opportunity and he must have seen how vulnerable she was. He *must* have.

She found herself wondering what would have happened if he *had* pounced. *Would* she have been able to resist him? She rubbed absently at her hair with the towel. Of course she would! She would be able to do anything she pleased, just as long as she had conviction!

She looked at the luminous face of the clock-radio and yawned. It wasn't as late as it seemed but she felt almost boneless with fatigue. She would try to sleep for a while and when he called to take her down to dinner she would politely tell him no. Yes, she would.

She padded over to the bed and pulled back the coverlet, slipping between the deliciously crisp, clean sheets, topped with a soft drift of blankets. Her mind was buzzing so much that she knew she wouldn't be able to sleep. But she closed her eyes anyway, and in her dreams she was still wearing Drew's ring, and it felt good, and the next thing she knew was the shattering shrill of the telephone, right by her ear.

She picked it up, disorientated and disappointed—aware that she still hadn't got to the best bit of the dream, though she wasn't quite sure what the best bit was. 'Hello?' she said groggily. 'Who's this?'

'This is your alarm call, kitten.'

She yawned; it was the rich velvet voice from her dream. Still half-asleep, she said, 'Mmm!'

'Mmm, what?'

'Mmm, what time is it?'

'It's nine o'clock.'

'What, in the morning?'

'No, Shelley. Still the evening. And the night is young.'

She looked down at the clock for confirmation and then to the window facing her bed. She hadn't bothered to draw the curtains and the evening sky was an inky-dark backdrop, studded with the pale points of stars.

'Hungry?' he questioned.

'Starving,' she admitted.

'And you're going to have dinner with me?'

'Isn't it too late to have dinner?'

'We're not *quite* that provincial down here,' he commented drily.

'What happens if I say no?'

'I don't know,' he mused. 'Consider the alternative.'

'Peace, you mean?'

'I don't think so, Shelley. The reality would be a table set for one, with everyone in the dining room wondering why such a beautiful woman was eating alone.'

The beautiful woman comment pleased her far more than it had any right to. 'But earlier you told me that I looked awful.'

'Well, you did. But I'm sure you wash up well,' he answered blandly.

'I could always have a tray sent up to my room.'

'Oh, come on—you'd spend the whole evening regretting it. Your heart just isn't in it, Shelley. Admit it!'

She wanted to tell him that he knew nothing about the contents of her heart, but she felt too sleepy and warm and comfortable to be able to compose something clever enough to dazzle him. And what would be the point of making a less than clever remark that he could easily obliterate with his caustic tongue?

And he was right. Her heart *wasn't* in it. She was only human. The luxurious life she had shared with Marco was now over. She had one night at the Westward and one night only—there would be plenty of meals on trays in front of the television in future!

This would be the most fabulous opportunity to demonstrate her new-found sense of purpose—and to show Drew that loose ends would be tied only if she wanted them to be tied! That she was grown-up enough to resist him. Hadn't she worked in one of the busiest art galleries in Milan, and resisted gorgeous men by the scoreful? 'I'll meet you downstairs,' she told him briskly. 'Give me half an hour.'

'I'll be waiting,' he said softly, and put the phone down.

She dressed, if not to kill, then certainly to maim. He had seen her at her very worst—now let him see the woman whom the exacting Marco Nero had been proud to escort to some of the most glitzy social functions in Italy!

First, her make-up. She set it all out on the dressing table like an actress dressing for a part.

Her skin needed practically nothing in the way of foundation, for it still carried a light tan, but she rubbed in a little concealer to get rid of the shadows underneath her eyes. It would be early nights after tonight, she decided grimly, brushing the heavy lids with a slick of silver colour and adding two coats of mascara onto the long, curling lashes. The result was startling. Starry aquamarine eyes sparkled back from the mirror.

Next she slid on wisps of lavender-coloured underwear—a vivid underwired bra which gave her a show-stopping cleavage and a wispy little suspender belt with panties which matched. She turned her head to look at her rear view, and wriggled her lace-covered bottom experimentally, thinking that she co-ordinated very nicely with the room! Softly sheened stockings and strappy, high-heeled black shoes and she was almost ready.

She knew exactly which dress to wear—the one which made her feel both attractive and unselfconscious. It was dark grey and starkly cut, and merely hinted at the body beneath—but there was no doubt that it was a very sexy dress indeed—in a cool, understated kind of way.

She took a final glance in the mirror. Her newly washed hair had fallen into place now—with the highlights and lowlights merging to create one glorious, shimmering whole. She picked up her bag, locked the door behind her, and went downstairs to find Drew.

The red-headed woman on the reception desk in the oak-panelled hall had been replaced by a sleek-looking young blonde.

'Ah!' She looked at Shelley with interest. 'Miss Turner?'

'That's me!' answered Shelley. 'I'm impressed! Do you know *all* the guests by name?'

'Of course we do,' said the blonde smoothly. 'We only have twelve rooms. Mr Glover said to tell you he's waiting in the restaurant.'

'Thank you.' *Mr* Glover? Why did the blonde say his name with the kind of reverence she might have used if the President of the United States was eating dinner in her restaurant?

But as soon as she saw Drew seated at the window table she wondered why she had bothered asking herself a question which was so fundamentally easy to answer.

The blonde had spoken like that because, quite honestly, he looked like a million dollars. In fact, it took a moment or two for her to recognise him, but judging from the slightly bemused expression on *his* face it seemed that the feeling was mutual.

Shelley blinked as he rose to his feet. He looked…well, he looked…unbelievable. Not just handsome. Not just strong. Or dependable. He looked *smart*. *Drew Glover looked smart!*

'Hello, Shelley,' he murmured, looking with wry amusement at the stark grey dress she wore. 'What's this—school uniform for big girls?'

'I don't know if the designer would be very pleased to hear you say that!' She stared at him. 'You've changed.'

'So have you.' His eyes narrowed at the expression of surprise on her face as she examined his suit close up. 'Were you expecting me to eat in a place like this—' and he jerked his head in the direction of the other tables '—wearing jeans and an old T-shirt?'

A waiter appeared from out of nowhere and pulled her chair back, and Shelley slid into it, taking the leatherbound menu he offered her with a smile of thanks. But instead of running her eyes over the starters she found that they were still riveted on the man sitting opposite her.

'I'm just not used to seeing you all dressed up,' she said slowly.

'You haven't seen me for two years,' he pointed out. 'And you still haven't told me whether you like it.'

Like it? It was a bit of a shock to see such an essentially outdoor man wearing a jacket and tie and a pair of navy trousers which seemed to emphasise his long legs even more than the jeans had done. And the outfit was exceptionally well made, she noticed with surprise. So Drew no longer bought his suits off the peg. Had she thought he looked like a million dollars? Make that a million and a half!

'Er, yes,' she said stiltedly. 'It looks very…um… smart.'

'Damned with faint praise!' he murmured.

'Oh, dear! Does your ego need constant massaging, then, Drew?' she enquired sweetly.

Their eyes met.

'Not my ego, no,' he told her deliberately.

Shelley flushed and leaned across the table. 'Let's get one thing straight, shall we?' she said, in a low voice. 'I may be in need of a square meal—but I'll walk straight out of here and order toasted cheese in my room if you continue to make references to sex all evening!'

'Sex?' he enquired innocently. 'Who mentioned sex? I thought we were talking about my ego?'

'Well, it's certainly big enough!'

His mouth twitched. 'Shelley—'

'Don't even *say* it, Drew!'

He sat back in his seat and studied her. Her blue eyes looked as big as a fawn's—she didn't really need mascara, but then she never had. 'I was right,' he said. 'You *do* wash up well.'

'Why, thank you.'

'Right—that's the flirting out of the way.' His eyes glittered. 'Now what shall we talk about?'

Shelley raised her eyebrows. 'Flirting? Is that what we were doing? Rather an unsophisticated version of flirting, I would have thought.'

'I bow to your superior knowledge, of course,' he said mockingly.

To Shelley's everlasting relief, the waiter appeared. 'Are you ready to order, Mr Glover?'

'Not quite. Give us five minutes, would you, please?'

The waiter went away again and Shelley quickly picked up her menu, then looked over the top of it into a pair of sapphire eyes. He certainly seemed at ease in such a lavish setting. 'What is it with the Mr Glover bit?'

she asked him. 'They seem to know you pretty well here. Don't tell me you're a regular, Drew?'

'You'd find that surprising, would you?'

'Well, yes, I would—to be honest.'

His eyes were questioning. 'Because?'

'Well, it's very expensive, isn't it? And I know that you make a good living from carpentry, but...' Her voice tailed off, slightly embarrassed, and he gave her another bright, searching stare which somehow had the ability to make her feel very uncomfortable indeed.

'But I'm not Bill Gates, right?'

She shrugged. 'Right!'

He slitted his eyes. 'Like I said—I've done a lot of work for them over the years—and that's how they know me. In fact—' and he lowered his voice by a fraction '—they give me a discount, too!'

'Oh, I see!'

He smiled thinly. 'So mind you look out for my handiwork!'

She looked around the restaurant. It was full, which was surprising for a Sunday evening in October. Even more surprising was the fact that Shelley didn't recognise one face in the place. Not one. And people were dressed in clothes which she instantly recognised as costly. A bit like Drew's, she realised. It looked more like a big-city restaurant, she thought in surprise, than one perched on an isolated part of the south sea coast in a small village.

'I don't recognise any locals in here either,' she observed.

'They're not. People travel some way to eat here. Great food, great view—with enormous beds upstairs should the urge take you.' He looked at her deliberately. 'What more could you ask for?'

Shelley began to look around the room with an air of

quiet desperation. This wasn't going to be as easy as she had thought.

'Anyway—I can tell you've worked here,' she said brightly.

He raised his eyebrows. 'Really?'

'Of course I can! Somebody's obviously been slogging their guts out on the place—and you always *were* a brilliant craftsman! This hotel always had the potential to be beautiful, but it needed lots of tender loving care spent on it. Now there has been, and it shows. Why, I expect they could almost employ you here full-time, couldn't they, Drew?'

He seemed to be struggling between controlling his temper and controlling his laughter. 'Have you any idea,' he asked eventually, 'just how patronising you sound?'

She looked at him in surprise. 'Patronising?' she echoed. 'How on earth would that be patronising?'

He gave a small shake of his head. 'Doesn't matter. Here comes the waiter. What do you want to eat?'

Slightly bemused by the tone of his voice, Shelley glanced down at the menu. She noticed that she had been given a copy without any prices. *Very* slick. 'It all looks good,' she commented approvingly. 'Small and simple.'

'What were you expecting after Milan? A list of out-of-season food which was obviously destined for the microwave before it reached us?' he enquired cynically.

'You're being very defensive, Drew!'

'I wonder why?' he mocked, then smiled at the waiter. 'I'll have the soup followed by the roast cod and chips, please. Shelley?'

'Chef's salad and a plain grilled sole, please,' she answered automatically.

'Scrub that. She'll have the same as me,' he told the waiter. 'You know how women fuss so much about their weight! So unnecessary—particularly in your case, kitten.' And he winked at her expansively across the table.

'Yes, Mr Glover!' The waiter smiled conspiratorially and scribbled the order down.

Only good manners prevented her from arguing the toss, but once the waiter had gone Shelley felt like hurling the contents of the bread basket at him. She leaned across the table towards him. 'I can't believe you just *did* that,' she hissed. 'But then I'd forgotten just how overbearing and domineering you could be!'

'Don't make a scene in public,' he answered mildly.

'Well, you started it!'

'Trust me.' He looked at her. 'When did you last eat?'

She thought back. 'I had breakfast.'

'Which was what?'

'The usual. Fruit and yoghurt.'

'Exactly. And since then you've driven from London to Milmouth, walked on the beach, had the trauma of going to your mother's house, driven up here, bathed—'

'You really *have* been spying on me, haven't you, Drew?'

He ignored that. 'You can't function properly if you don't give your body the fuel it needs.'

'What's *wrong* with my body?'

'I told you before. It's too skinny. Now drink a glass of this.' And he poured out a red wine which smelt enchantingly rich and powerful.

Shelley took a sip. It was.

'Better?'

'A bit,' she answered grudgingly as she felt herself beginning to relax.

'Now.' He leaned back in his chair and looked at her. 'Where do we start?'

She heard the slight edge in his voice and looked down

at her cutlery, deliberately misunderstanding him. 'I think
you just work from the outside in.'

'*Very* amusing!' He studied her from across the table.
'Though I suppose it wouldn't surprise you if I picked
up my soup plate and started slurping from it?'

'Oh, there we are on the defensive *again*!'

'Only with you, kitten—only with you.'

She sighed and reached out for a bread stick. 'Just tell
me what you want—'

'In full and aching detail?'

'Though maybe it's time I told *you*.' She snapped the
bread stick cleanly in half and saw him wince. 'Shall I
explain exactly what happened that night with Marco?'

'Why? Do you think it will change things?'

No, she didn't. Not change things in a fairy-story kind
of way. But maybe change the way he felt about her.
Eradicate some of the contempt. 'What did you *imagine*
happened, Drew? It was an innocent evening, followed
by an innocent kiss. That's all.'

'That's all?' The blue blaze of his eyes lanced her like
a javelin. 'But you lied, Shelley. You lied to me. Didn't
you?'

'Yes, I did!' she admitted. 'But think about *why* I lied!
Because I was afraid of what you'd say if I told you the
truth! I should have had the courage to do that, but I
didn't. And don't you think that says a lot about the
inequality in our relationship, Drew? That I didn't dare
tell you I had made a stupid mistake?'

She had run from Marco's car and into her mother's
house as though there had been demons on her heels.
Which she supposed there had. And her mother had come
downstairs to ask her what on earth was going on,
alarmed when she saw Shelley's white face.

'Shelley, what's happened? What's *wrong*?'

'*Nothing's* wrong!' Shelley snapped. '*Nothing!*'

'But—'

'Just leave me alone, Mum,' she begged. 'Please.'

Shaking uncontrollably, she locked herself in the bathroom and stripped all her clothes off and washed every bit of her body, scrubbing at her skin with soap and tepid water, like a punishment.

But the clothes felt tainted—she knew that she would never be able to wear them again. She stuffed them into a plastic bag and was just bundling them into the garbage when a tall figure appeared from out of the shadows in front of her.

She started with guilt. 'D-Drew,' she stumbled.

'What's the matter, Shelley?' His voice sounded low, soft, deadly. She had never heard him speak like that before.

'N-nothing's the matter,' she answered, much too brightly.

'Really? But your face is very white, and look...your hands are shaking.'

'Well, it's...it's cold.'

'Yes, it is,' he agreed. 'Far too cold to be putting the rubbish out, surely?'

She should have come clean then. Should have blurted out the truth and taken all the disdain and condemnation he was prepared to throw at her. Then maybe she would have earned his forgiveness. But she was frightened. Frightened of what she had done and how Drew would react if she tried to explain that one mad moment of stupidity. So she did the worst thing possible.

'Oh, well.' She licked her lips nervously. 'I just wanted to help my mother.'

'How sweet.' There was a pause. 'What are you throwing away?' he asked casually.

Shelley jerked. 'What?'

'You heard me. I asked what you were throwing away.'

And she made the lie a thousand times worse by attempting to put him down. 'Surely you aren't interested in the contents of my garbage bin, Drew?'

'So you're not going to tell me?'

'Drew!' Her heart was hammering.

'Let me see.'

'Drew—'

'*Let me see.*'

She turned away, her heart thumping so painfully that she thought she was about to die. But she didn't hear the rustle of plastic as Drew withdrew the package she had just put in the bin, and she turned round again to find that he hadn't moved. Misplaced hope made her look at him optimistically, praying that she had been given another chance.

As soon as she saw his face she knew that her prayers had not been answered. It was dark and demonic, condemning and cruel—and her own crumpled in response.

'Yes,' he jeered softly. 'Infidelity. It's written all over your face as clearly as if you'd marked it with an indelible pen.'

'I can explain—'

'Explain what?' he demanded coldly. 'Explain that you went off with your fancy Italian playboy?'

'Drew—'

'Went drinking with him? Flaunting yourself at the Westward with him?'

'It wasn't *like* that—'

'Like what? Like what everybody told me?'

Shelley gave a silent sigh of relief. So he hadn't seen

her for himself. Oh, thank God. It was bad enough, but at least it could be rectified.

'And that he bought you champagne and fed you olives with his fingers? And that you sat there, giggling like a girl of fifteen—'

'Instead of an old woman of nearly twenty-one, you mean?' she flared back at him, stung at the loathing which had hardened his face. 'Whose fiancé keeps her on a leash?'

He carried on as if she hadn't spoken, and by losing some of its fire his voice had become even more dangerous, even more destructive. 'And then he drove you back here in that *monstrous*-looking car of his—'

'You're just jealous!'

'Of his car? I don't think so. A man usually buys a car like that to compensate for certain...how shall I put it...*inadequacies*. You know what they say—big car, small...' He let the unsaid word hang on the air, insultingly. 'But you would know about that, wouldn't you, Shelley?'

'What the hell are you talking about?'

'Oh, come on! Please don't insult my intelligence by trying to play the innocent with me! I *saw* you! Okay?' His voice shook. 'Saw you with my own eyes!'

'You...*saw* me?' she stumbled in frozen disbelief.

'Yes. Saw the way he was kissing you. I was standing watching, and it's burned on my memory, kitten—'

'Then you will also have seen that I jumped out of the car,' she defended. 'Won't you?'

'Oh, sure,' he agreed. 'Because I don't think that even you would be so brazen as to have sex in the car in full view of your mother's and your fiancé's house!'

'You're mad! Completely mad!'

'Yes, I think I must have been,' he agreed evenly, only

now there was something unrecognisable in his eyes which made her heart lurch with fear. And excitement.

'Drew,' she said warningly, only she could not work out what the danger was.

'What?' he answered softly. 'What is it?'

He pulled her into his arms and drove his mouth down onto hers in something which could never be described as a kiss. Not if a kiss was supposed to be a gesture of mutual desire and caring. Oh, the desire was there, all right—but nothing in the way of caring.

'Drew!' she gasped, through the hot anger of his breath.

'What?' He ground his mouth down harder and pushed his hand up underneath her sweater to roughly cup her breast, running his thumb across the nub with a fire and a fury that made her body cry out for his possession. And Shelley was appalled to feel her knees sag.

'God, you're really turned on, aren't you?' he breathed. 'Did he get you all hot for me, kitten?'

She opened her mouth to object but he had pushed her up against the wall, kissing her little moans of protest away until they became tiny yelps of pleasure. And then his fingers were trembling at her denim skirt, buttons flying open, and his hand was splayed hotly on her thigh as he pressed against her urgently. Desire soaked her as she felt him hook her panties with an impatient finger, and then suddenly he made a choking kind of sound, and tore himself away from her, his breathing sounding like someone who had been starved of air for more than three minutes. Someone who was nearly dead.

And something *had* died.

She knew straight away what it was. The love which had always glittered in his eyes when he looked at her. And Shelley could have fallen to her knees and wept.

He couldn't speak for a moment and when he did he destroyed the last, lingering trace of hope.

'You sicken me,' he managed at last. 'You sicken me beyond belief. Go to your rich lover, Shelley. Go give him what he wants. What you seem to want more than anything. Certainly more than decency and respect—' And he turned on his heel and left as abruptly as he had arrived...

Shelley looked at him now, through the candlelight which danced on the table before them. 'You were so harsh and unforgiving, Drew. Don't you know that I had to summon up every bit of nerve to come round to see you the next day? To make my peace?'

'You had wounded my pride,' he said simply. 'Incapacitated me with your lies. I was afraid of my temper, afraid of what I might say, what I might do...'

Jennie had come to the door, her face sour with disapproval.

'Can I see him, Jennie? Please? To explain?'

Jennie shook her head, struggling to come to terms with what she had obviously just been told about her best friend. 'He won't see you, Shelley. He's made his mind up. He says he won't ever see you again.'

'Here—' Tearfully Shelley began to tug the thin gold band with the tiny diamond from her finger. She wrenched it off. 'You'd better give him his ring back!'

'He won't want it.'

'Then tell him to melt it down! Or to keep it—to remind him of what a lucky escape he had!'

Word filtered out around the village, and even her mother found it difficult to speak to her without looking as though she was going to be ill. She was whispered and talked about on the streets and several of the bolder youths from the housing estate made it very clear that her reputation had gone before her.

Even Geoff, who had sold Marco the car at a substantial profit, was disapproving, but then he liked Drew. That was the trouble. Everyone did.

Shelley felt isolated and marginalised and at the end of her tether. In despair she fished out the heavy ivory card which Marco had given her. He had written a London phone number on the back.

'If you want to see me,' he had purred, 'then give me a ring.'

She took the train up to London, feeling lost and very small in the noisy, bustling capital. And feeling very out of place in her cheap clothes when she met Marco in a hotel which was the last word in luxury.

They sat together in the foyer and he seemed to notice her uneasiness as she stared indifferently at the bone-china cup of tea which stood cooling before her.

'Let's go for a drive,' he said suddenly.

He drove her out of town and parked the car by the river, and she told him everything that had happened. Afterwards they sat there in silence.

'So what do you want to do?' he asked eventually.

'I don't know.' Was that disorientated little voice really hers?

'And you say it's definitely over? Between you and this Drew?'

'Definitely,' she said flatly. 'He saw us.'

He said something in Italian and Shelley didn't speak a word of the language at the time, but even she could work out that he was swearing.

'Would it help if I spoke to him? If I took responsibility? Told him that things got a little out of hand, but that it was nothing more than that?'

'Only if you want to get your face beaten in.'

He put his hands on the steering wheel. He wore leather driving gloves which were as soft as skin. Gloves which probably cost as much as Drew's entire week's salary.

'And you are a virgin.' It was more of a statement than a question.

'Yes. Yes, I am.'

A sigh escaped from his mouth. She saw his hands grip and tighten around the steering wheel, saw the brief nodding of his head as he seemed to come to some sort of decision.

'Let me tell you a little about myself,' he said softly. 'And afterwards you must decide whether you want to come to Italy with me.' He turned, and gave her a blinding smile. 'Mustn't you?'

To a young and mixed-up girl, it had seemed the only solution.

'Madam?'

Shelley looked up. The waiter had arrived with their first course. She kept her gaze fixed on the swirl of cream and chopped herbs which topped the soup, and it was seconds before she could find the courage to lift her face and look directly at Drew.

Did he see her pain? Her regret? Was that why he was studying her so intently, as if uncertain of what she would do next?

'It hurts to remember,' he observed.

'Of course it does.'

'Didn't you realise,' he questioned softly, 'that coming back to Milmouth would bring all those memories back? What did you think it was going to be like, Shelley?'

'I don't know. I didn't stop to think. But even if I had

I think I would have come anyway. I can't keep running away from the repercussions of what I did. It's time I faced up to them and let them go. Maybe it's time to bury the past, Drew—once and for all.'

'And how are you going to do that?'

'By accepting that I probably hastened my mother's death...' Her breath caught in her throat. 'She was heart-broken by what I did—'

'No, Shelley!' he put in fiercely. 'There are plenty of things you *can* beat yourself up about—but that isn't one of them. Your mother's death was premature, yes, but natural—the doctors all said so!'

'But I didn't come and see her for a year!' she moaned. 'And when I did it was too late—she was lying in a coma and couldn't hear me!'

'You couldn't have predicted that would happen!' he argued. 'I went away from home for *three* years, remember? Something similar could have happened to me, but it didn't. You were just unlucky.'

'Yes.'

'Hey!' he said softly.

She looked up at him. 'What?'

'Your mother got over your defection, you know, Shelley.' His smile was almost gentle. 'Mothers always do—once they realise they can't plot out their children's lives for them.'

'You can't know that!'

'Yes, I can—because she told me.'

'Did she? Really?'

'Really,' he nodded.

'Oh.' Some of the burden lifted from her shoulders. 'I'm still sorry for what happened,' she said simply. 'And for the way it happened.'

He gave a short laugh. 'Me, too.'

'I should have—'

'Shh.' He shook his head and the candlelight emphasised the honeyed gleam which tipped each dark strand. 'We can't change anything by wishing we'd behaved any differently. We just have to deal with what really happened.'

'Oh, Drew!'

He looked at her thoughtfully. 'Eat your soup, Shelley,' was all he said.

He didn't say another thing as Shelley began to steadily eat her soup with the air of someone who had only just realised what hunger meant. Words would distract her, and she didn't need any more distractions, not at the moment. Right now she needed to eat.

He didn't know what he had expected to feel about her. Over the years he had anticipated many reactions when he saw her again. *If* he saw her again. He had never been able to count on that, despite his own gut feeling, despite what her mother had once said to him. His favourite response to her had been one of complete indifference, but even in his most furious moments of denial he had known that one was a non-starter.

His imagination had given her and the Italian at least one child together. And an idyllic relationship—in the way that other people's relationships always looked idyllic. Frustration and hurt pride had subsided over the years, until they could be filed away as experience. He had convinced himself that he was well rid of the bitch.

Yet life was never that simple. Something inside him had flared when he had seen her today on the beach, her fingers bare of rings. So was that simply lust? Fuelled by absence and the fact that he had never tasted her body in the way which had haunted his dreams for as long as he could remember?

'Oh, that was *good*!'

He watched as she finished the soup and put her spoon down, looking up at him with a glowing face which made her look about sixteen years old. Or seventeen...

'You haven't even touched yours,' she observed.

'No.' He didn't want it. He had lost his appetite. Or rather he'd lost that particular appetite. Another—sharper and much more intense—was raging inside him like a wild storm right now. 'It's grown cold. I think I'll skip.'

Shelley nodded and ate some bread, and he watched while the life and the colour came back into her cheeks.

'So tell me about Milmouth,' she said. Anything to distract him, to stop him from staring at her like that. Because she was feeling the strongest urge to push back her chair and grab him by the hand and pull him to his feet and... 'Has it—er—changed at all?'

He smiled. 'What's this? Distraction technique?'

'It's called making conversation!' she snapped, thinking how perceptive he was.

As opposed to making love, he thought ruefully, before he remembered. If he and Shelley *did* get physical, it would not be termed making love—not by anybody's definition. Not now, and not after all that had happened. It would be explosive, probably amazing, and certainly shattering—sex. That was all.

'Well, we have a good general store now, which is trying—and largely succeeding—to attract customers away from the big out-of-town stores. And there are a lot of arty-crafty people moving in—'

'To Milmouth?' she asked, surprised.

'Uh-huh. There's now a craft shop in the old bakery, which holds workshops in the winter months. You can make silver jewellery or learn to paint. And there's a very good vegetarian restaurant—one of several new restaurants which have opened up. The down-side is, of course, that house prices are going up. But people seem to be opting out of stress-filled city life.'

'And coming to Milmouth?' she asked in surprise.

'Why not? And speaking of opting out—did you know that Geoff sold the car showroom?'

Shelley shook her head. 'I wasn't really in Geoff's good books when I left. What's he doing now?'

'Would you believe he's bought an organic farm?'

'*Geoff?*' Shelley giggled. '*Very* trendy!'

'And very successful, apparently.' He looked at the way the candlelight flickered over her face. It was odd, this slotting into relaxed ways—feeling comfortable sitting at a table with her. Finding that talking to her was still as easy as a summer's morning. Surely it shouldn't still feel like that?

'So Milmouth's the place to be?'

He nodded. 'Easy to see why—it's an exquisite location, right by the sea, and it's relatively inexpensive.'

'Those are precisely the reasons I'm here myself,' she agreed pensively.

'Oh, Shelley!' he mocked. 'Didn't I even enter into the equation?'

'Yes! And nearly put me off coming back at all,' she told him truthfully, wondering why that should cause him to smile.

He joined in with the food once the fish arrived, but drank only coffee while Shelley ploughed her way through a portion of chocolate mousse and cream.

'Wow! When you break a resolution you really go for it, don't you?' he remarked softly.

She searched his face for hidden meanings, but there were none and she realised that the evening had passed in a pleasant blur. Apart from that bit at the beginning, they hadn't really gone in for recrimination and heavy analysis. Thank the Lord. She didn't think she could have taken it—it would have been too much coming on top of everything else.

'Like some coffee?'

Shelley yawned. To be honest the food had provided a distraction as well as filling the gaping hole of hunger. It had been easier to put her head down and plough through the soup and that delicious fish than to have to meet that ocean-blue gaze head-on. And now she had eaten so much that she felt she must have gained at least ten pounds! She felt that her legs would barely be able to carry her back upstairs.

Which was good. She wanted to hit that pillow and just crash out. It was not on her agenda to lie awake half the night tossing and turning, unable to get Drew's face out of her mind.

He saw her flagging and was infuriated by the sudden surge of protectiveness which washed over him. He guessed that old habits died hard. He would do the same for any woman who looked ready to drop, he told himself. 'You look like you're ready for bed,' he murmured.

It was perhaps unfortunate that the way he said it made it sound full of sexual intent, and that a well-preserved woman in her forties who was passing their table on the way to the powder room heard him. She must have done. Why else did she ogle him, before raising her eyebrows slightly and passing Shelley a look of shrugging envy?

Shelley bristled at the implication. 'I suppose you think that for the price of a discounted meal in a fancy restaurant I'm just going to fall straight into bed with you, do you, Drew?'

Her voice carried more than she had intended, or perhaps there was just a natural lull in the general low-pitched hubbub of the dining room. Whatever the reasons, the room grew silent and she could feel the eyes of every person in the place—bar the few people who were too polite to turn their heads—looking at them.

He studied her from across the table with eyes which were chilly now. 'That isn't my usual *modus operandi*, no. But maybe it's yours. After all, isn't that precisely what happened all those years ago? Only he got away without even having to buy you a meal!'

She glared at him, not caring about the interested faces of the other diners as she began to fumble around in her handbag. 'I should never have agreed to eat with you! Or did you think that saying you wanted us to be equals gave you the go-ahead to just sit there insulting me?' She pulled out her purse and caught the waiter's eye, trying to calm her rage as he hurried over to their table. 'Can we have the bill, please?'

'Now what do you think you're doing?' growled Drew.

'What does it look like? I'm paying my share of the bill, of course!' She extracted a couple of crisp notes. 'That way no one owes anyone *anything*! And certainly not in the bed stakes! Got that?'

The waiter was looking at Drew in a perplexed kind of way. 'But Mr Glover usually settles—'

That did it! Shelley was appalled at her reactions and even more confused about their origins, but seemed helpless to stop herself from slamming the notes down on the table in front of him and leaning forward to demand, 'Why? Just how many women do you generally bring here in the space of a week, *Mr* Glover?'

Drew laughed, suddenly elated. 'And what's it got to do with you, kitten?'

She frowned suspiciously. 'In fact, you've hardly

talked about yourself all evening. If we're talking enigmatic—you fit the description pretty well!'

He smiled. 'What did you want me to talk about?'

'Well, where are you living, for a start?'

There was a brief pause. He had wondered how long it would take her to get around to asking. 'In the old coastguard's cottage.'

Her mouth fell open as if someone had twitched a string on a puppet. That was to have been *their* home—not his! 'You mean you went ahead and bought it anyway?'

He raised his eyebrows. 'Yes, of course I did. That had always been my intention. Or did you imagine that my pain was so great that I wouldn't be able to lead an ordinary life there? That I'd be too haunted by memories of you?'

She knew that she was being unreasonable, selfish and illogical, but she couldn't seem to stop herself from asking questions to which he was probably going to provide the most horrible answers.

'And have you taken other....?' She *couldn't* ask.

'Other?' he enquired helpfully.

'Women!' she got out at last. 'Have you taken other women there?'

A nerve flickered in his cheek. 'What an audacious and arrogant question, Shelley. I can't believe you had the nerve to ask it! You've been living with another man for the past three years—so what do you expect? Yes, of course I've taken other women there! Or did you really imagine that I spent night after night alone, dreaming of my lost love?' He raised his eyebrows sardonically. 'Dream on, kitten!'

'Oh!' She levered herself to her feet and picked up her

handbag and tried to think of something really, really withering to say.

But those mocking blue eyes somehow took the wind right out of her sails and so did the fact that he had scraped his own chair back and was rising to his feet as well, big and dark and menacing. And suddenly the vulnerability was back. She had to get away.

'I'll see you to your room.'

'Don't bother.'

'It's no bother,' he smiled, but there was no disguising the glint in his eyes.

'This is harassment!' she gritted.

'It's all a question of interpretation, surely?' he countered. 'Let's just call it etiquette, shall we, for the sake of argument?'

It seemed a mile to the door and into the panelled hall, but there was no sign of the blonde at the reception desk.

Shelley put one spike-heeled shoe on the foot of the staircase. 'Don't you dare come any further!' she warned.

'Why? Don't you trust yourself?' Unexpectedly he reached out his hand and captured her wrist, pulling her towards him, his other hand slipping down to the small of her back, so that she was enclosed and supported by him.

Standing on the step in her high heels meant that they were exactly the same height. His face was right up close, close as this afternoon's dreams which had so tantalised her, blue eyes blazing with a passion she couldn't tell was benign or malevolent. And the temptation to melt against him was intense.

She fought it. 'Let go of me, Drew.'

His voice was a low, mocking caress. 'Say it once more, kitten—only this time with meaning!'

'Let me...*Drew*!' He had dipped his head to her neck,

a feather-light brush of his lips against the pale skin there, and Shelley trembled. 'Oh! Don't.'

'Why not?' His mouth had drifted to the line of her jaw, a brief stroking of velvet-soft lips there, more seductive than anything had a right to be. 'Feels good, doesn't it, kitten?'

It felt absolutely gorgeous, that was the trouble—but this was no innocent little kiss goodnight—despite what it looked like. She knew what he wanted—the tension in his body was almost palable, even from here—and he was barely touching her. Yet.

She wound her arms around his neck and put her face even closer, so that to an outsider it looked as if she was returning the embrace, while the duel being fought in their eyes told another story. 'If you don't let go of me right now,' she told him in a low voice, 'then I shall be forced to adopt tactics of self-protection which I guarantee you will not like. Certain parts of the male anatomy are extremely sensitive to rough handling!'

'Is that what Marco used to like you to do?'

She didn't react. 'I enrolled in a course of self-defence in Italy, if you must know. Do I make myself clear, Drew?'

'Perfectly.' He let her go with an aching smile. 'I can see I'm going to have fantasies about being roughly handled by you, Shelley.'

'In your dreams!'

'That's exactly what I meant,' he mocked. 'Men have been having dreams like that about women since time began!'

She opened her mouth to snap back some smart comment, but the little spark which smouldered blue flames at the back of his eyes told her that she was playing with fire. 'Be as outrageous as you like,' she told him sweetly. 'You won't shock me!'

'Is that an invitation?' he murmured.

'No, it is *not*!' But she wasn't giving him the chance to test her resolve.

'Pity,' he remarked, watching her prepare to take flight. 'And you should be careful how you walk on those outrageously high heels, kitten.' But he was still smiling as she scrambled up the stairs to her room, two at time.

CHAPTER SEVEN

IT WAS nearly ten when Shelley woke up in the most comfortable bed she had ever slept in, feeling like a different person. Even after the shock of discovering that Drew had obviously taken women—she wouldn't let herself even try to estimate how many—back to the home which they had once both intended to share, she had still slept.

And maybe her subconscious had done her a favour during the night, because this morning she realised that he had been absolutely right. It *had* been an arrogant and audacious assumption on her part—to suppose that he had slept with no one. That didn't stop it hurting, of course, but at least she could accept it. That was what being a mature person was all about...

At the open window, the breeze made the silky lilac curtains rustle and billow, so that they floated like a dancer's skirt. She stretched extravagantly and got out of bed, stepping over the clothes which she had left where they had fallen. She had tumbled exhausted into bed last night—without even bothering to brush her teeth and take her make-up off. What on earth would Marco say? One day back in Milmouth and she was turning into a slut!

She went into the bathroom to repair some of the damage done overnight, wincing at her panda eyes and pale face, but once she'd showered and dressed she felt like a new woman. The blonde from the evening before was back on duty at the reception desk, and gave Shelley a helpful look of enquiry.

'I suppose they've stopped serving breakfast?' Shelley asked.

'They have,' the girl nodded. 'But you can order a snack from the bar lounge, if you like. Or I'm sure that Chef would be happy to rustle you up something from the kitchen.'

'Could you arrange to have fruit and yoghurt and a pot of coffee sent up to my room? I need to make a few phone calls.'

'Certainly, Miss Turner.' The blonde smiled back. 'Any idea how long you'll be staying with us?'

From out of the corner of her eye, Shelley noticed the impressive symmetry of the minstrels' gallery. Above her head glittered the most flamboyant chandelier she had ever seen. Someone had spent a lot of time and money making this place beautiful, and she dreaded to think how much it must be costing her to stay there. Still, Marco had always paid her generously. And she could probably run to a few more nights until she got the house settled. Of course, only a fool would do that without checking first and she had already behaved foolishly over the water and electricity.

'I'd better have a look at your tariff first, hadn't I?' she said, only half jokingly.

The blonde looked slightly taken aback. 'Well, I don't expect you'll be paying for your room.'

'What do you mean?' Shelley smiled as she glanced down at one of the very glossy hotel brochures. 'Has a new law come into being since I've been living in Italy? Don't tell me! You've started offering free board and lodgings?'

'Well, only sometimes!' The blonde giggled, and then Shelley could have sworn that she almost winked.

Shelley frowned. There was something vaguely troubling about the other woman's attitude towards her, something reminiscent of the way people used to treat her when she went to hotels with Marco. A kind of envy. She had understood why in *those* circumstances—he was a rich, eligible man and she was his partner. But not these. 'I'm not sure that I understand,' she said slowly.

The blonde had started to look worried now. 'I shouldn't have said anything. Honestly, it doesn't matter!'

'Oh, but I think it does,' Shelley asserted. 'Why on earth would I not have to pay for my own room?'

The blonde coloured. 'Oh, heck! Look, I'm sorry. I certainly didn't mean to cause offence. It's just that— well, the boss made such a fuss before you arrived yesterday—he went around inspecting the place as if we were entering the Hotel of the Year competition!'

Shelley registered what the girl was saying, but one word alone stood out and blasted its way into her subconscious.

Boss.

Boss?

She stared very hard at the receptionist. 'Who exactly is your boss?' she asked, even though something told her she already knew the answer.

The blonde bit her lip. 'Mr Glover. Drew Glover,' she enlarged unnecessarily.

'And he's the manager of this hotel?'

'The manager?' The blonde blinked her lashes rapidly and nearly raised a smile at this. But not quite. 'Oh, no-o-o, he's not the manager! He *owns* the hotel. Well, a part share. The *biggest* share, actually,' she confided, and this time she *did* wink.

'He owns it?' Shelley recited dully. 'This hotel?'

'Oh, yes!'

'Anything else besides?'

'Such as?'

'Well, he hasn't bought up the local golf-course while I've been away? Or the boatyard at Milmouth Waters?'

'Oh, no!' laughed the blonde. 'But he's got quite a few properties dotted around Milmouth. He has a reputation for being something of a wheeler-dealer in these parts.'

'Oh, does he?' questioned Shelley faintly.

The blonde had started to look really worried. 'Only we weren't supposed to say anything—not to you. That was the whole point. He told Dee—she does the opposite shift to me—'

'The redhead?'

'That's right!' The blonde nodded her head worriedly. 'He told her that no one was to let on to you that he was anything other than an ordinary punter. That there was to be no fuss. I just thought that this morning...'

'This morning what?'

'I can't!' The blonde shook her head. 'Mr Glover'll *kill* me,' she breathed.

'Only if I tell him. I might decide not to.'

The blonde looked at her hopefully. 'Why would you do that?'

'In exchange for a little information.'

'What kind of information?'

Shelley glanced down at the woman's name-badge, then fixed her with a steady stare. 'What were you expecting to happen this morning, Moira?'

The blonde blushed. 'Well, I thought he might have told you about himself some time during the night.'

Some time during the night. The words reverberated round her head, heavy with implication. Shelley stared at the girl in horror. 'Are you implying that Mr Glover and I spent the night together?'

The blonde looked as though she wished a trap-door would open up for her to disappear through. 'I didn't mean to cause any offence—honestly, I didn't. It's just that you didn't come down for breakfast, and we haven't seen *him*, and someone said you looked very close at dinner last night, and so I put two and two together—'

'And came up with five hundred and forty-five?' suggested Shelley drily.

'Oh, heck!' Moira moaned. 'Why didn't I just keep my big mouth shut?'

'I'm very glad you didn't.' Shelley heaved out a long breath and the question which followed it was not one which should have been number one on her agenda. 'He has women to stay here a lot like this, does he?'

'Oh, no! He has a reputation for being picky,' the girl revealed. 'Women throw themselves at him all the time— I suppose that's not very surprising when you think about it. But he's ever so choosy.'

'Is he, now?' asked Shelley, more grimly than she meant to, but took pity on the blonde's abject expression. 'Listen, I think I'll pass on breakfast. I'll just nip up and pack my bag, and while I'm doing that I'd like you to total up my bill for me.'

'But I can't do that!'

'Why not?'

'He's written ''G'' at the top—see?'

'And ''G'' stands for?'

'Gratis!' said Moira helpfully.

Free! Shelley felt so incensed that she had to clench her fists by her sides to stop herself from howling with rage. 'Just work out what I owe, will you, Moira?' she said quietly.

She was back in minutes, having thrown everything she'd unpacked into the overnight bag, and she wrote a cheque for the amount she owed, resisting the desire to deface it with insults.

She left the bill on the reception desk, and was almost at the door when she saw Moira waving it in the air. 'Don't you want your copy, Miss Turner?' she enquired anxiously.

Temptation lifted its provocative neck and Shelley succumbed to it. 'Give it to Mr Glover, will you?' she said. 'Tell him that I would suggest a use for it, but I'm sure he can work out for himself what that is!'

She drove like the clappers back to the house and was getting out of the car when Jennie came outside, as though she had been watching for her. Shelley's first thought was that she really shouldn't wear those yellow checked trousers. They did her bottom no favours whatsoever. Next time Jennie went shopping, maybe she would ask if she could tag along.

'How was the Westward?'

'Fine,' said Shelley shortly.

'You look all strung out,' Jennie observed. 'What's the matter—didn't you sleep?'

'On the contrary. I slept like a log—'

'So I suppose it's safe to suppose that my brother wasn't with you?'

'Just what is it with your brother?' Shelley exploded. 'Is he such a stud that when any woman with a pulse walks into his life the whole world thinks he's sleeping with her?'

'You *were* engaged to be married, Shelley, remember?' Jennie reminded her gently. 'And I came knocking on your door yesterday, remember *that*? The sparks between you two were flying so hard that I was half afraid I was going to combust when I walked in!' She frowned.

'Well, if Drew isn't responsible for those tight lips—what's the matter?'

Shelley considered her options. She was planning to have a very serious word with Drew. If she asked Jennie about his connections with the Westward, then she might very well report back to her brother. Which would spoil the element of surprise. What did they say? Forewarned is forearmed. And she certainly wasn't going to do him any favours like *that*.

'Oh, I've decided that I can't keep swanning around the place as though I'm on holiday,' Shelley told her blithely. 'So I've come back here to get things kick-started.'

Jennie grinned. 'Good! I've been without a neighbour for too long!'

'Could I use your phone to get on to the water and electricity people?'

Jennie waved her arm in the direction of her front door. 'It's all yours! And it's past mid-day. Why don't you stay and have some lunch with me, or did you have a late breakfast?'

'I'd love lunch—I'm absolutely *starving*!' said Shelley smoothly, neatly avoiding the reason why.

She followed Jennie into the house on exaggerated tiptoe. 'Should I whisper?' she asked, doing just that. 'Is the baby asleep?'

Jennie shook her head and smiled. 'No. Drew has taken her out to the beach.'

Some invisible force whacked her hard in the stomach. 'Drew has?'

Jennie's smile widened. 'Well, don't sound so surprised! He dotes on her! He's wonderful with her, too—and Ellie thinks that he is the most fantastic person in the entire history of the world!' She glanced down at her watch. 'I'll go and make some lunch. The phone's over there. Help yourself.'

'Thanks.' Putting annoyingly persistent thoughts of Drew being wonderful with babies right out of her head, Shelley flicked through the directory until she found numbers for the electricity and water boards. Then spent a frustrating ten minutes on the phone to each of them before replacing the receiver and collapsing on the sofa with a yelp of exasperation.

'Trouble?' asked Jennie mildly, coming into the room carrying a tray which held a plate heaped high with sandwiches, and a bottle of wine.

'Bureaucracy,' Shelley scowled. 'Need I say more? Apparently, they can't get either of the services connected until the end of the week because of some stupid system of priority! The end of the week—I ask you!'

'Oh, dear. Here—' Jennie handed her a glass and filled it '—drink this, it'll make you feel better.'

Shelley groaned as she took a mouthful. 'Mmm. It does.' She sat upright and assumed an expression of horror. 'What's happening to me, Jennie? Last night I went to bed still wearing my make-up and now I'm drinking wine at lunchtime!'

'It's a long, slippery slope!' Jennie agreed gravely. 'And do you know what I'd do in your situation?'

'You'd leave town, or crawl under the bedclothes and pretend none of it was happening?'

'Nope. I'd get Drew onto the case.'

'Drew?' questioned Shelley darkly. The secretive, controlling Drew, she wanted to add, but resisted. Even if a brother and sister fought like cat and dog, there was still such a thing as sibling loyalty. And she couldn't really remark to Jennie that Drew was the person she was least likely to ask for help about *anything*. Not until she knew what reasons lay behind him taking her to *his* hotel, and pretending he was just Joe Ordinary. And oh, hadn't she fallen for it—hook, line and sinker?

'Mmm. He works miracles with stodgy officials—has them eating out of his hand!'

Enough was enough! 'Oh, stop making him out to be such a saint!' said Shelley crossly. 'I thought he was stopping you from being together with Jamie! What about his dark, controlling side—why don't we talk about *that*?'

Jennie looked down at her untouched sandwich. 'He says he only wants the best for me.'

'Well, he *would* say that, wouldn't he?'

'He…'

Shelley stared at Jennie's anxious face. 'Tell me,' she urged gently. 'Go on—you're bursting to get it off your chest, aren't you?'

'I guess so,' Jennie sighed. 'Well, when Jamie and I…' She bit her lip as the words trailed off.

'When you and Jamie what?' Shelley prompted softly. 'Is it that you've split up but can't bring yourself to say the words out loud? Because saying them only rubs in that they're true?'

Jennie looked at her in surprise. 'Why, yes—that's exactly it. How did you guess?'

Shelley pulled a face. 'How do you think, Jennie? And it wasn't a guess—I *know*—I've been there! People may have me down for Little Miss No-Heart, but I can assure you that I was…' She remembered just who she was talking to and amended the sentence '…sad.' Yes, sad was a good word—it implied calm, measured emotion, which had certainly not been the case at the time. A feeling that the most vital part of her had been torn out of her body without anaesthetic was closer to the mark. 'I was very sad—when my relationship finished.'

'You must have loved him very much?'

'I…yes, of course I loved him. I loved him—' her voice began to falter and she realised that in a minute she would blurt out her fear that she still did '—very much.'

'Your face went all soft and dreamy then.' Jennie's voice was wistful. 'I suppose there's no chance that the two of you could get back together?'

Shelley shook her head. 'No. None whatsoever. If he wants me at all now, it's just for sex—'

'And that doesn't interest you?'

'Well, I'm only human. Of course it interests me! It just won't lead anywhere—so it would be sensible to avoid it, wouldn't it?' She wriggled her shoulders a little bit and gave a polite smile, the way people did when they wanted to close a subject. It didn't really seem appropriate talking about Drew this way. Not to his sister. 'Now tell me all about Jamie.'

Jennie refilled their glasses. 'The pregnancy wasn't planned—' She looked up and met Shelley's searching gaze. 'Well, that's not strictly true.' She blushed.

'You were careless?'

'I loved him,' Jennie explained simply. 'And I just couldn't get worked up about using contraception. Next thing you know, there's a baby on the way.' She sighed. 'Jamie didn't find me very attractive when I was pregnant, and then couldn't cope with the baby crying all the time when she was born. He's not much older than me, you see,' she added, as if that explained everything. 'We were living in Jamie's tiny bedsit, and I seemed to be crying all the time, too—'

'I'm not surprised!' Shelley pulled a wry face. 'Stress

and wildly fluctuating hormones do not make a harmonious combination.'

Jennie stared down at her wine glass. 'That's when we split up. I didn't really want to leave, but I could tell that me staying was just making things worse for everyone.'

'And how old was Ellie at the time?'

'Five weeks.'

'*Five weeks?* He let you go when you had a baby of five weeks to look after? What kind of man would do that?'

'Funny.' Jennie locked and then unlocked her fingers distractedly. 'That's exactly what Drew said.'

'I'm not surprised! I'm not your brother's greatest buddy, but I have to say that I think his character assessment was spot-on there.'

Jennie shook her head. 'It isn't like that! And Jamie isn't like that! Things have been much better between us since I left!'

'Well, of course they've been better!' Shelley scoffed. 'For *him*! He gets all the best bits of having a girlfriend and a baby, with none of the noisy, tiring, smelly bits! It's known,' she added gently, 'as having your cake and eating it.' She saw Jennie's stubborn expression, and sighed. She had it bad. 'So what happened?'

'Drew persuaded me to move in here. The house was empty and he owns it now. He bought it off my folks so that they could buy somewhere on the Isle of Wight— though I was surprised he kept it on. I mean, it's hardly a palace!' She looked around the room, as if seeing it for the first time. 'Maybe it was just sentimental of him, but it's lucky for me he did. Anyway, he had it all decorated and made it cosy for me, but—'

Shelley swirled the wine around in her glass. Italian wine. 'But?'

'He won't let Jamie move in here with me. He says that it's time Jamie stopped being spoon-fed.'

'And does Jamie want to move in here?'

'Oh, Drew's been so difficult about it that he says he doesn't know *what* he wants any more, apart from his boat.'

'So let me get this straight...' Shelley frowned. 'Jamie has a child he doesn't support and a boat he does?'

'No!' Jennie shook her head. 'It isn't like that! He *does* support Ellie—and he has to work very hard in order to do that.'

'Well, that's what most of the people on this planet do,' Shelley pointed out gently.

'But Jamie's brilliant with boats! He's a natural—everyone says so. And there's a beauty for sale down at Milmouth waters—only she's been terribly neglected. Jamie's dying to work on her and the owner's given him first refusal. And it's such a wonderful opportunity!' For a moment her face screwed up with enthusiasm, like a child's. 'If he could just buy this boat and do it up, the profit we'd make selling it would set the three of us up. It *would*!' she added fiercely. 'We could buy this house from Drew. Or buy another instead.'

'But Jamie doesn't have the money to go it alone, and Drew won't help him?' Even though it now transpired that Drew had become Mr Money-Bags. Control freak, thought Shelley brutally.

'That's it in a nutshell, yes.'

'So you've reached a kind of stalemate?'

'Yep.'

'Let me give it some thought,' said Shelley. 'Though I'm not really qualified to advise other people how to run their lives.'

'Yes, you are!' said Jennie fiercely. 'At least you've

seen something of the world! And lived in Italy! I've never set foot outside Milmouth—unless you count a fortnight's holiday in Spain when I was fifteen!'

Shelley laughed and drained her glass, realising that it was her second. Which might explain the sudden flushing heat to her cheeks. The whoozy feeling in her stomach. 'Wow!' she puffed. 'I'm not used to drinking at lunch-time—it's gone straight to my head!'

'Have one of these sandwiches.' Jennie passed the plate. 'I know they look like doorstops, but they make great blotting paper!'

Shelley was just demolishing her second when the doorbell rang, and Jennie got to her feet. 'That'll be Drew and Ellie—so bye-bye peace and quiet!' she sighed. 'Because much as I love my daughter to pieces it's wonderful to be able to sit and have this slightly decadent lunch without having to leap to my feet every five seconds!'

'I can always babysit—if you want to get out with Jamie one night. Or afternoon. Name your day!'

'Do you mean that?'

Shelley laughed. 'Of course I do! Listen, if Drew's here I'd better go.'

'No, don't go, Shelley—he'll be pleased to see you.'

Shelley smiled, but didn't argue, and as soon as Jennie had left the room the smile vanished from her face and she sat upright, hearing the deep voice in the small hall-way, and straining her ears to hear what they were saying.

Jennie must have told him she was there, because his face was dark and watchful when he walked in. The chubby baby was clinging onto him like a baby chim-panzee, with her soft, dark head snuggled close to his neck, and Shelley felt a sudden pang, and if she had analysed it and described it to another woman they would immediately have come up with the correct diagnosis.

Broodiness.

She stared at him. Oh, but he looked good holding a baby!

Drew slanted her a look as he saw her sitting bolt upright on the edge of the sofa, the dark lashes veiling the brilliant sapphire glitter of his eyes. He took in the hectic flush of her cheeks and her over-bright expression. 'Been drinking?'

Her cutesy image of him dissolved like sugar. 'Well, what do you know—Detective Glover has arrived! Have I been drinking? he asks. What does it look like? Oh! It's all gone! So no, Drew—I'm not drinking at the moment, but that's easily remedied!' Shelley held up her empty glass and rather defiantly refilled it. 'And before you say anything—I'm not drunk!'

'Just a little merry?' he queried as he began to unzip Ellie's play-suit. 'With the intention of getting completely legless before the afternoon is out?'

'I'm not even merry!' she defended, sagging back against the sofa. 'Quite the opposite, in fact!'

'Well, you soon will be if you carry on knocking it back like that.'

'Da-*da*!' squealed Ellie, and tugged at a stray lock of dark hair.

'Ouch!' he protested, unlocking the plump little fingers from their vice-like grip. 'And I'm not your daddy, kitten!'

'It's just a thing they say,' said Jennie, coming into the room and holding her arms wide open to her daughter. 'Just a sound they make—it doesn't mean anything!' She held her nose closer to Ellie's posterior. 'Think I might have to go and freshen this child up! Help yourself to wine and sandwiches, Drew!' She spotted the empty bottle and grinned over her shoulder as she carried Ellie out. 'Open some more, if you like!'

'No, thanks,' he drawled. 'I've got things to do.'

'Like spinning another elaborate pretence, I suppose?' questioned Shelley maliciously. 'Like making out you're still a simple jobbing carpenter when you've obviously joined the ranks of the super-rich?'

'I'm not quite in that league yet,' he offered drily. 'I meant like getting your electricity and water connected, actually. Jennie said that you're going to have to wait until the end of the week.'

'That's what they said.' She glared at him suspiciously. 'And I don't see how you're going to change their minds when they told me most definitely that it was non-negotiable.'

'Well, why don't I give it a go?' he queried calmly. 'Come on—let's walk next door and we can tell them what it says on the meters.'

'But I haven't got a *phone* connected next door,' she said in an irritated voice. In fact she felt *very irritated indeed*—surely far more than was reasonable? 'Remember?'

'Well, it's your lucky day, Shelley—because I've got one right here.'

With a lazy smile he inched his hand slowly down from the waistband of his jeans and Shelley's eyes widened with horrified anticipation as she wondered just what he was going to do next.

Until she suddenly realised that he was sliding his fingers deep down into the front pocket of his jeans to extract a slim mobile phone.

He held it up like a trophy. 'See?' He plucked the wine glass from her hand and deposited it on the table. 'Leave that. You don't need any more.'

Infuriatingly, he was right. Not only didn't she need any more—she didn't want any more, either. In fact, she was beginning to feel quite sick.

Determined not to betray even the slightest wooziness, Shelley rose to her feet, as upright as a toy soldier.

'Shelley and I are just going next door!' he called upstairs to Jennie.

Outside, the sky was a clear bright blue, the air all crisp and fresh—while the sun gilded the small suburban houses into doll's-house palaces. Once they used to have the run of each other's houses—and Shelley found it achingly evocative as she remembered how their twin lives used to merge into one.

'Key!' He held his hand out like a surgeon and Shelley found herself obediently handing it over, and he unlocked the house.

He held the door open for her, and she had to pass with breathtaking closeness to him. She found that she couldn't look him in the face. The house screamed out its silence, and its emptiness made Shelley gulpingly aware that they were all alone...

She dared to raise her eyes at last, to discover that he wasn't watching her at all, but was already poking around in the hall cupboard to find the meter and was punching out numbers on his mobile phone.

She listened with fascination, disbelief and finally incredulity as Drew managed to get himself put through to people further and further up the system—first at the Water Board and then at the Electricity Board. And when he'd finished he slid the phone back into his jeans and grinned.

'Sorted! They'll be here by the end of the afternoon.'

Shelley was aware of a great, gaping hole of insecurity which made her pathetically ungrateful for his help. So that instead of thanking him she found herself sniping, 'You think you're so clever, don't you?'

He shrugged, half modestly. 'Well, you don't have to be clever to beat the system, Shelley—just have persistence and confidence with a little gift of the gab thrown in for good measure.'

'And you've certainly got those three in abundance, haven't you?' she snapped, trailing into the sitting room, her heart beating even faster when she heard his footsteps behind her. 'You'd have to be amazingly confident to go to the trouble of telling your staff to *pretend* that you didn't own the Westward! And you must have told Jennie to join in with all the subterfuge, too—'

'She didn't want to,' he confessed. 'But I made her promise.'

She narrowed her eyes at him. 'And what prompted all this intrigue, I wonder, Drew? Not modesty, surely?'

He leaned negligently against a piano which had not been played for years. 'Not modesty, no. Just a desire to see whether you'd changed.'

'Whilst maintaining the pretence that you hadn't?'

'To be honest, I rather enjoyed being patronised by you, Shelley—it made a refreshing change. Women can be so *obvious* once they know you have money.'

Now why did it feel as though he was twisting the knife when he said something like that? Something told her that she was walking straight into a trap, but the wine had made her reckless. 'How obvious?' she asked. 'A throwing-their-knickers-at-you sort of obvious?'

She saw the fractional darkening of his eyes, the crooked grin which made him look like a roguish kind of pirate, and again felt the dull ache of regret.

'Mmm,' he purred. 'Unfortunately that hasn't happened yet.' He lifted his eyebrows in a kind of mocking question. 'Of course, I live in hope, Shelley.'

His murmured words tugged at her with stealthy sorcery, and desire unfurled inside her like a bud in spring. She folded her arms across her chest, which didn't really help at all. It was supposed to be a gesture of self-protection and defiance, but all it succeeded in doing was making her painfully aware of the tingling fullness of her breasts.

She thought about Marco's gallery in Milan—the must-see place of the fashionable city. So what interested little question would she ask a man in whom she had no emotional interest? She would curve her lips into a polite half-smile. She did so. 'And how did you manage to acquire the Westward in the first place, Drew? Did your Premium Bonds come up, or something?'

'There's that superior little voice again,' he mocked. 'How it does a man good to eat a little humble pie now and again—particularly when it comes from such a delectable source!'

'No, seriously. I'm interested.'

'Oh, well, if you're *interested*...' His mouth curved into a lazy smile. 'Who told you, by the way?'

'Told me what?' she enquired innocently.

'So you've learnt to play the tease?' He gave a half-smile of rueful acknowledgement. 'That I owned the Westward?'

Shelley kept her promise to the blonde. 'Oh, come off it—how long did you honestly think you could keep something like that a secret for? I was bound to find out sooner rather than later!'

'Which neatly answers the question, while not answering the question at all,' he mused. 'Very loyal of you, Shelley. Funny, that; I didn't think that loyalty was a quality you rated very highly.'

'I asked you a question which you were in the process of answering,' she pointed out testily. 'If you could just put your character assassination of me on hold!'

Still half sitting on the piano, he stretched his legs out in front of him, completely distracting her, in spite of her determination to remain unmoved. It would take a woman of steel not to be affected by that endless dazzle of faded denim, stretched tautly over his thighs.

The slight smile which hovered around his lips indicated that her ogling hadn't gone unnoticed. 'You want to know how I made my money?' he mused. 'There's no secret. Just plain hard work with an added bit of luck— the usual way.'

'You make it sound so easy?'

'No, not easy. Simple, yes—but not easy.' He smiled. 'It may surprise you to know that all the day-release and night-school classes which took me away from you so much finally paid off. I realised that people paid a hell of a lot more for having their houses *designed* rather than for having them *built*. And the thing that set me apart from my competitors was that I could do both.'

Her eyes dilated. 'You mean you actually design houses now?'

'Well, I *can*. I have done. Sometimes I still do. But I do other things, too.'

'Such as?'

He suddenly looked rather pleased with himself. 'I call it reinvention. It started when I bought a repossession on a mortgage. Got the house dirt-cheap and I thought I'd just do it up and sell it on. But it occupied a vast plot of land—so I applied for planning permission and built another house at the bottom end of the garden. The challenge was in making both houses look wonderful and complete and not as though someone had just lopped the garden in half—'

'Which you did, I suppose?'

He shrugged, and then grinned. 'Yeah, I did. Then I sold them on—two for the price of one.'

'And made a big profit?'

'Huge. Don't look so surprised, Shelley.'

'I can't help the way I look! I suppose you invested the profit?'

He shook his head. 'Not in the conventional sense, no. Houses are about the best and safest investment there are—but not many people have the skills to make the best of them. Fortunately, I do. So I carried on. I bought various properties—one here, one there. One might need an extension, another a new kitchen—a big house might need a granny annexe. I put in loft extensions and conservatories and earned a reputation for *sympathetic* additions—and that was what did it. If people think you're going to create something which is both well made *and* beautiful—well, you're onto a winner. I even learned to landscape gardens.'

So he still had that driven work ethic. 'And all the time you were getting a big return on your money?'

'That's right,' he nodded, and rubbed his chin with a thoughtful thumb and forefinger as he watched her reaction. 'When John Cutliffe grew tired of running the Westward, he was very particular about who he sold it to. He wanted someone he knew would love the building. Someone who would preserve and care for it. The oak panelling in the hall badly needed the attention of a carpenter, and that was just for starters. John wanted reassurance that the new owner wasn't going to blitz those exquisite stained-glass windows and put ugly replacements in their place.'

'I can see why he chose you,' she said truthfully.

Suspicion touched the thoughtful features. 'Why, thank you, Shelley,' he murmured. 'Praise from you is always welcome, if a little unexpected.'

Her suspicion matched his. 'But you've obviously spent *masses* making the Westward look so beautiful. Hasn't that eaten into your profits?'

'What's the matter, kitten? Worried that the coffers have all dried up? That I'm rich in assets, but not in cash?' He pre-empted her indignation with a shake of the honey-tipped head. 'I realised that the place was not being used to its full potential. Milmouth is too far off the map to rely on being fully booked all year round—and I didn't just want to open during the summer season. So we started specialising in celebrations. Weddings are our big thing. But we do birthdays, too, and we hire the house out for corporate use sometimes, if the price is right.' He pulled a face.

'Those aren't my favourites,' he admitted. 'Corpulent businessmen getting drunk and trying to pull the receptionists!'

'Oh,' said Shelley faintly.

'We bought our very own Rolls-Royce, which is driven by our very own chauffeur. Brides like to travel in style,' he grinned. 'Then I hired a chef fresh out of college who has proved inspirational—he was featured in one of the nationals last month. Plus we now have year-round employment for our workers—it doesn't stop when the summer ends.'

'Quite the knight in shining armour, aren't you?' she sniped. 'Do you rob the rich to pay the poor?'

He smiled. 'That was Robin Hood—and he wasn't a knight. I think you're mixing your metaphors, kitten.'

'Gosh, you seem to know something about everything, these days, Drew! And all without the benefits of a university education!'

There wasn't a flicker of response. 'Do I detect a note of bitterness beneath the sarcasm? Perhaps of regret?'

She hoped he couldn't read her lying eyes. 'Regret?' she said lightly, and even managed a disbelieving laugh as she shook her head. 'No.'

'No?' He had moved away from the piano and was standing just in front of her, and Shelley found herself shying back from him, like a nervous horse. 'That's not what your body language is saying to me, Shelley.'

'I don't know very much about body language!'

'Well, I do—'

'So I hear! Especially *female* body language!'

He stilled. 'Don't talk in code, Shelley,' he said softly. 'Say what you really mean.'

It hurt. That was the stupid, crazy, illogical thing about it. It hurt like mad. 'I gather that women fling themselves at you in locust-like numbers—but that you're very choosy!'

'So?'

She realised that she had run herself into a tight corner. She looked at him. 'I don't know.' She shrugged helplessly.

He looked angry then. No, not just angry.

Seething.

The explosion, when it came, was quiet and deadly. 'Do you really think that you can break off our engagement—'

'You *forced* me to break it off!'

'—to go swanning off to Italy with your rich lover and

live with him for *three years*—so it doesn't exactly fall in the category of brief fling, does it?—and then come back here and start acting like a betrayed wife—as though you have every right to?'

Some inner need to know and to torture herself made her ask, 'So have you?'

'Have I what? Made love to hundreds of women?' he grated. 'Do you want names and dates while we're on the subject?'

She clapped her hands over her ears, completely forgetting that they had been covering her aching breasts for a reason. 'No!'

'No, that's right!' he agreed roughly, his eyes riveted to the straining swell. 'There's only one thing you want right now, isn't there, Shelley? And you're just crying out for it.' He pulled her into his arms, as she had known he would. Prayed he would...

He dipped his head to speak softly into her ear. 'Like I said, kitten—your body language speaks volumes.' His mouth moved from ear to neck with painstaking precision. Barely touching her when, quite frankly, if he had thrown her down onto the carpet and then, weighted himself on top of her she would have cried out with pleasure.

He placed his hands loosely at her shoulders—so no one could have said that he was holding her against her will. Because he wasn't. He wasn't. Oh, Lord—his mouth was brushing across her cheek now, and she was restlessly turning her face so that he could capture her lips and he was laughing at her, mocking her.

And finally, when their lips fused, the pleasure was so intense that it was like lights going off inside her head, sparks igniting in her veins. Coupled with the honeyed tug of desire, it was the most devastating cocktail imaginable. And he had always been able to do this. Bring her to this earth-shattering brink within minutes.

The hands moved from her shoulders with lazy deliberation towards her breasts. She could have stopped them. Stopped them before they started playing idly with the tips so that she moaned. And then prevented him from cupping them luxuriously, measuring their weight like a connoisseur, even though she hated to think of his expertise in this area. Pain fused with pleasure, making it even more intense.

Feeling the hot, sharp pull of surrender, she pressed her body against his in blatant and unashamed need, when he abruptly pulled away from her, his face full of bitterness as he stared down at his shaking hands.

'God, it's so true!' he said, as if he was talking to himself. 'It's so bloody true! The predictability of women in general—and you in particular!'

She stared at him, shook her head in confusion, too baffled for words.

'Last night you wouldn't come near me!' he accused hotly. 'You looked like I was guilty of a capital crime when I tried to kiss you! Did you still see me as your poor, jobbing carpenter with no ambitions other than to keep a roof over his head?'

The unjustness of the accusation stung her. All her life she had wanted him, no matter how much he had—or didn't have—in his wallet. 'You know that's not true!'

'Do I?' He shook his head. 'All I know is that today you've discovered that I'm worth something and you can't wait to fall into my arms like a windfall—overripe and juicy—just waiting to topple from the tree. Are you overripe and juicy, kitten? Want me to find out?'

The insults fired her up, his scorn and obvious dislike giving her back her power of speech. And pride. 'You?

You think you're worth so much? Well, I'll tell you exactly what you're worth, Drew Glover—*nothing*! Nothing at all!'

'But you couldn't wait for ''nothing'' to engage in a vigorous bout of sex with you, could you, Shelley?'

She burst out with a high, nervous laugh. 'You make it sound like a boxing match!'

'Then tell me how *you* like to describe it, kitten,' he suggested, on a silky threat.

And his question brought it crashing home to her how completely his love for her had died. Oh, he still felt desire, strong desire—yes—he had made that *very* clear. But what was desire without respect? Wouldn't that just chip away at her self-esteem, and risk destroying it completely?

'Your new-found wealth seems to have affected your judgement,' she told him coldly. 'You have become even *more* high-handed and right now I could almost hate you, Drew Glover!'

'Maybe you could—but you still want me all the same, don't you, Shelley? Just the same as I want you.' His voice was like silk, his words rich and dark and sultry, and she could feel the tension between them gathering momentum, like a snowball rolling down the side of a hill.

'You'd better get out before either of us does something we might really regret,' she warned him.

'I think I just have! I stopped *before* the home truths. I should have waited until afterwards—and at least that way I might have got you out of my system once and for all!'

And he slammed his way out of the house before she had time to think of a suitably crushing reply.

CHAPTER EIGHT

THE resumption of power supplies to the house gave Shelley a feeling of having some control back in her life. It was just slightly galling that she had Drew to thank for the speedy arrival of men in vans wearing overalls.

'It's very sweet of you to come out so quickly,' she ventured to the man from the Water Board.

He shrugged. 'Drew Glover drinks with the boss—what do you expect?'

Guilt at the inequality of life nagged her. 'That's terrible!'

'Not for you, it isn't!' The man grinned at her, and looked around curiously at the house. 'You're going to be living here, are you?'

The tone of his voice told her what he really meant—that she looked all wrong in a tiny semi, wearing her sleek designer clothes. And he was right.

'For the time being,' she said, aware that she was making her mind up as she answered his question. 'But I'm going to decorate, first. Then decide.'

'Yeah,' he agreed. 'The place could do with it!'

She spent the rest of the afternoon and most of the evening scrubbing the house from top to bottom and fell into bed exhausted after eating beans on toast. To her great pleasure and even greater surprise, she had a dreamless and Drew-less night's sleep. Maybe she was slowly working him out of her subconscious. Maybe…

The next morning, following a delicious hot bath full of childhood memories, Shelley walked into the village centre to buy groceries and a newspaper. It was a cool, misty morning and in the distance the sea looked all fuzzy and indistinct, like a grey mohair scarf lying on the shore, stretching as far as the eye could see. The sea drew her like a magnet, and she decided that she would go for a bracing walk *before* she bought her shopping. If she had heavy bags to carry she knew she wouldn't get round to it.

She peered into the windows of the shops as she passed, noticing that there was nothing which catered for clothes of either sex…not even a baby boutique. She wondered if the new-look Milmouth approved of that.

She was dressed more appropriately today in an outfit which was casual and warm. She had hung the linen suit at the back of her wardrobe where she suspected it would remain unworn. At least for the time being. In the meantime she found a pair of black jeans and a black sweater in her suitcase, which were the most suitable things for facing a blustery sea breeze.

Admittedly, the jeans were designer-made so they were cut to flatter rather than to stride around in—and a costly cashmere sweater wasn't the best thing to wear if you were pottering around the house! But they were the best she could come up with and obviously she was going to have to invest in some new clothes. Maybe she would suggest that shopping trip to Jennie soon.

The sky was grey and smoky and rain didn't look very far away, but Shelley took a chance, and walked along the shoreline, filling her lungs with great breaths of salty air. Beneath the mist, the sea was the colour of mercury and the tips of the waves were crested with bubbles like bath foam. Seagulls circled overhead like low-flying aircraft, and in the far distance she could see the slow, stately movement of a ship.

She walked until she was pink-cheeked and glowing and told herself that she was free to explore where she wanted—and that if her path took her through the sand-dunes and past the old coastguard's cottage, then so be it. Drew might own half the Westward but he didn't own the beach yet!

As she approached, she thought that it was a little like childhood in reverse. Instead of being smaller than she remembered, the cottage looked about twice the size, and closer inspection soon showed her why. It *was* twice the size, but the extensions had been so carefully constructed that the entire building somehow retained that look of being there for centuries. Clever, she thought grudgingly. Very clever.

It was long and low and whitewashed, and the window frames were all painted a deep delphinium-blue. The garden was beautiful—with tall, billowing grasses and the blue-green blur of lavender bushes which blended so well with the landscape. The pale frothy flowerheads of hydrangeas blew gently in the sea breeze and she could see small, silver-leaved plants and the maroon fronds of a Tamarix.

But there was no sign of Drew.

She told herself that she was relieved not to have seen him as she walked slowly back to the village centre and pushed open the door of the general store. And she told herself that again as she looked around her appreciatively.

The shop had been deliberately designed to look as though you were stepping back in time—to a time when provisions were wholesome and processed foods rare. Except that it now sold olive oil from Tuscany, which was comparable to the fruity blend she used to buy in her local market in Italy! On the floor were great sacks of coffee beans, filling the air with their dark, bitter scent—along with all kinds of dried mushrooms, and boxes of exotically flavoured biscuits. And bread which looked hand-baked, and cheeses from local farmhouses— not the tasteless blocks she had been used to as a child, which had looked like soap and tasted like soap!

The man who served her was called Charlie Palmer, and he chattered away and told her that he owned the shop. He looked about thirty-five, and wore the wedding ring and comfortable smile of the happily married. He filled up three boxes with all the basic foodstuffs she needed, then added fresh eggs and some organic meat which he had talked her into buying.

'Oh, heavens!' groaned Shelley, wondering how she was going to carry everything home. 'I've bought more than I meant to! And I haven't even started on my fruit and veg yet!'

'I trust you're buying them next door, and not from the out-of-town superstore?' He gave her a humorous frown.

'Oh, I am! Definitely!'

'Well, if you bring it all in here, I can deliver later, when I shut up shop.'

She smiled at him. 'That would be wonderful! And very kind of you.'

He smiled back. 'It's a calculated kindness. That sort of service gets me custom. People don't mind paying a little bit more if they get the personal touch—and who in their right mind would want to do their shopping in a place the size of an aircraft hanger?' He pulled a face. 'Where do you live?'

She told him.

'Next door to Jennie Glover?'

Shelley nodded. 'That's right. Do you know her?'

'My wife does. We've got a baby the same age as Ellie. And, of course, I know her brother.'

'Do you?' asked Shelley casually.

'Yeah—I supply coffee and chocolate to the hotel.' He grinned. 'Oh, and Drew thrashes me at tennis occasionally, too!'

'Really?' Shelley decided to risk it. 'I didn't know that Drew played tennis?'

Did she detect a twinkle in Charlie's eyes? Was he, as his sister had once been, familiar with women asking him sneaky little questions about Drew?

'He only took it up a couple of years ago, apparently—and he's sickeningly good!' He wrapped a piece of cheese in greaseproof paper and looked up. 'Friend of yours, is he?'

Shelley spoke from the heart as she remembered the harsh way he had left her, and the bitterness of his parting words. 'Oh, no! *No.*' She saw Charlie looking at her as if she were slightly deranged. Or lying. 'Not buddy-buddy, not really. I just knew him way-back-when.'

'You grew up round here, then?'

'That's right. I've just…' She hesitated, having no desire to tell this man, however nice, her whole life story up until now. 'Come home,' she said simply.

She spent the next week in a flurry of activity, pruning the hedges at the front of the house and cleaning out all the cupboards inside. The garden at the back needed very little attention—thanks, she realised, with an odd little beat of her heart, to Drew. She stared out of the window at the Michaelmas daisies which were the exact colour of the curtains of the Lilac suite, and sighed.

She was persuaded by Jennie to go down to the boat-yard at Milmouth Waters to see Jamie hard at work. And to see the boat which he was desperate to buy.

Shelley had grown up by the sea, and recognised a beauty of a vessel when she saw one. Inside the cavernous interior of the boatyard, the *Misty Morn* was strong and hunky and yet elegant, too. True, she had been allowed to run down into a state of disrepair, but there was nothing that lots of hard work and love wouldn't cure.

She spotted Gerald O'Rourke straightening some rigging, the unlit butt of a cigarette clamped between his lips. He had been working round boats at Milmouth since the beginning of time—or so it seemed.

Shelley waited until Jennie had gone to chat to Jamie and give him a pack of sandwiches before she wandered over to speak to Gerald.

'Jamie seems to like boats,' she observed.

Gerald shot her a shrewd look. 'You an investor these days, then?'

She looked at him in surprise. 'No. Why d'you ask?'

He squinted his rheumy old eyes. 'He needs one, that's why. Wants to buy the *Misty Morn*, and she won't wait for ever.'

'But is he any good?' Shelley found herself asking.

'Hardest-working lad I've ever known,' said Gerald, shrugging.

So Drew was simply being stubborn about the money, was he? Shelley screwed up her nose in disgust, before reminding herself that it was none of her business. None.

She took the car to the large cathedral town of Southchester further up the coast, and bought tins of bright paints and brushes with a definite air of excitement. Giving the house a brand-new look would not only cheer her up in the short term, it should prove useful if she *did* decide to sell up.

She came back loaded with bags of shopping, including a pair of regular blue denims and a few cotton slouch sweaters which she'd actually bought in *colours*, having decided that maybe it was the time to stop wearing only neutrals. Here, against the sea-fresh atmosphere of Milmouth, the greys and blacks she had worn in Italy now seemed dull and self-limiting! And she had forgotten just how much she loved wearing blue!

She was out in her front garden planting spring bulbs in a large terracotta tub one morning, when Jennie came out of her front door and leaned over the fence.

'I haven't seen you all week!' she accused.

'Well, I've been here.'

'Why didn't you pop in?'

Shelley shook her head, and pulled a face. 'I'd hate you to think that I was the neighbour from hell—looming up on the doorstep every time you wanted a quiet five minutes!'

'Oh, come on! You know very well I wouldn't mind.' Jennie gave her a searching look. 'Is it because of Drew?'

Shelley's heart blipped. 'Is what because of Drew?'

'Is that why you won't come round? Because the two of you can't seem to make your minds up whether you want to kill one another or kiss one another.'

'But Drew doesn't live there, does he?' Shelley brushed some compost off her nose with the tip of her thumb.

'No, he doesn't! And please don't forget that!' Jennie seemed about to say something else, but looked down at the bulbs instead. 'They'll look lovely in spring.'

'I hope so.' She wondered whether she would be here to see them flower, or whether the reality of seeing Drew living his life without her would be too much to tolerate. 'My mother loved these tiny daffodils.'

Jennie nodded. 'I know she did. Um, Shelley—'

'Mmm?'

'You know you said you'd babysit for me some time?'
Shelley smiled. 'When do you want me?'

'Is tonight too short notice?'

'I've not exactly been snowed under with offers of
dates! I'd be happy to. Where are you going—somewhere
special?'

Jennie ran her hand through untidy hair which was
badly in need of a wash. 'Jamie wants to take me out
dancing—and we haven't done that since the baby was
born!'

'Mmm! Sounds promising. What time?'

'He's coming round about eight.'

'Well, why don't I come over earlier—say about
seven? Then I can help get the baby to bed, while you
glam yourself up.'

Jennie started blinking rapidly. 'I don't know how to
thank you.'

'Hey! It's nothing—honestly.' Shelley's voice was
soft. 'You're just at the mercy of those wretched hormones again, aren't you?'

When she arrived at Jennie's, the place was in chaos—
Ellie was screaming and there was a strong smell of burning—while Jennie herself was looking red-faced and pan-
icky.

'I left a pot of banana custard in the saucepan and
forgot to turn it off! It would happen tonight—of all
nights! And Ellie won't stop crying!' she moaned. 'I
can't possibly leave her!'

'Nonsense; of course you can!' said Shelley smoothly,
and gave the baby a delicate little sniff. 'She needs
changing, for starters, so I'll do that first. Has she eaten?'

'Just. Well, I tried—but she wouldn't take much.'

'Right.' She looked Jennie up and down with an ap-
praising eye. 'Have you had a bath yet?'

'No.' Jennie shook her head. 'And I don't know if there's going to be enough time—'

'Oh, yes there *is*!' interrupted Shelley firmly, not meaning to be overly critical, but thinking that this was what friends were for. And only Jennie's worst enemy would let her go out without washing her hair! 'Listen, I'll clean Ellie up and then bath her in the kitchen sink, while you have a shower. And make sure you wash your hair. Spend as long as you like getting ready—I can look after Ellie.'

'You're very confident around babies,' Jennie observed, stooping to pick up a rattle.

'Well, Marco had a lot of nephews and nieces and we often went to visit them,' explained Shelley, realising that Jennie was longing to ask her more. 'Go on! Leave that!' she grinned. 'Go and make yourself beautiful for him!'

Jamie was late. Not very—just by ten minutes—but Shelley was irritated. Lateness was a power thing, especially if the occasion was important—Marco had told her that.

When she'd seen him down at the boatyard, he had been showing off his body in a pair of jeans and a singlet, but tonight he was dressed up to go out. And he really was spectacularly good-looking, she thought.

He had been attractive as a schoolboy, but now he had blossomed into a real head-turner, with an over-long tumble of blond curls and tanned skin—and teeth which were so perfect that they could have been a set of dentures!

He was also an incorrigible flirt and his baby-blue eyes widened like a cat's when Shelley opened the door to him.

Then he made a great show of rubbing his fists against his eyes before looking at her again. 'Have I died and gone to heaven?' he said.

'The first part can easily be arranged!' she retorted. 'Though I wouldn't count on heaven as your destination!'

He laughed. 'You're so pretty.'

'No, I'm Shelley!'

He followed her inside. 'I didn't get a chance to speak to you when you came down to the yard. But I know who you are—your reputation goes before you.'

She turned around. 'Oh? From school, you mean?'

'No. As the only woman who has ever walked away from dearest Drew.' He said the name as though he didn't like the owner of it very much. 'And I can't think of anyone more deserving!'

She didn't want to talk about Drew with anyone—least of all with Jamie. 'Do you want to go and see Ellie?' she suggested. 'I can tell Jennie you're here.'

'I can tell her myself,' he said easily. 'Is she in the bedroom?'

Shelley had learnt many things in Italy—and one of them was that a woman should always maintain a certain air of mystery. Which roughly translated meant that it would be better for a woman to run naked in the streets than shave her armpits in front of the man she loved! She also suspected, from the slightly decadent look on Jamie's face, that he would take great pleasure in going upstairs to make love to Jennie, knowing that someone might be downstairs, listening.

'Don't worry. I'll tell her you're here,' she asserted firmly.

Jenny was sitting in front of the mirror, about to apply a coat of livid crimson lipstick, when Shelley walked into the room.

'Don't!' she yelled.

'Don't what?' Jennie paused. 'What is it?'

Shelley snatched the lipstick out of her fingers and

substituted it with a subtle pink sheen she had seen on the dressing table. 'Try this instead,' she suggested. 'It'll go with your dress and it's more subtle. Oh, and Jamie's here—'

Jennie sprang to her feet. 'Great!'

'Make him wait,' said Shelley, sitting her back down again, thinking it ironic that she knew exactly how to keep a man interested. And yet wouldn't dare try any of these ruses on Drew... 'While I blow-dry your hair for you.'

Jamie looked suitably impressed when Jennie swung into the room in a cloud of scent, her hair all glossy and neat and providing a perfect contrast to the short black dress she wore, with a sugar-pink cardigan.

She smiled shyly at Jamie, then turned to Shelley. 'There are phone numbers in the book,' she said. 'The doctor and Drew—both helpfully filed under "D"—but God forbid you need the former!'

Or the latter, thought Shelley, but didn't say anything.

'You look great, babe!' Jamie murmured in Jennie's ear as Shelley closed the door behind them.

And, while Shelley felt delighted at the glowy-eyed looks the two of them were sending to each other, a sense of her own loneliness hit her very hard.

She went upstairs to settle Ellie and found her tossing restlessly in her cot. She seemed a little hotter than she had done earlier. Mind you, the room was quite warm. But that was one good thing about these little houses—they had brilliant insulation!

Shelley took the blanket out of the cot, turned on the musical mobile, and, leaving the door open, she slipped out of the room and went downstairs to make some coffee.

But Ellie wouldn't settle. Shelley kept checking on her

whenever she made a squeak. And when she resumed a particularly miserable grizzling she went upstairs and found her lying on her stomach with her little bottom in the air, making a miserable whimpering sound.

'What's the matter, kitten?' Shelley whispered to her, echoing her uncle's favourite pet name.

Ellie whimpered.

Shelley carefully snapped the poppers on the sleepsuit and took it off, leaving her wearing just a little vest and nappy. But the baby started to wail loudly, and Shelley scooped her up out of the cot, startled to discover how much hotter she felt in her arms. Her little vest was soaked.

Oh, Lord—did she have a raging temperature, or was she just hot from crying?

Shelley carried her downstairs to the sitting room, cradling her over her shoulder. And the baby was violently sick all over her sweatshirt.

Shelley bit down the panic which rose inside her. She liked babies. She was good with babies. But well babies. Babies who cooed and gurgled and splashed around in the bath a bit and then went to sleep.

Not babies who were hot and bad-tempered and who had just deposited the entire contents of their stomach all over you.

She could…what?

Gingerly strip off her top before she bathed the baby? Except that she didn't want to put her down—not even for a moment.

Or bath the baby first? But then the baby would get all smelly again when Shelley picked her up in her own soiled clothes. And she was too little to sit up in the bath on her own. Besides which—what if she turned out to be seriously ill? How would she cope then? She wasn't a single mother—she didn't *have* to struggle on her own. She could pick up that phone right now and Uncle Drew would come haring over to help.

And it wasn't fair to make the baby suffer, simply because she and Drew weren't speaking. Was it?

With one hand on the baby, she punched out his number.

She thought he sounded sleepy when he answered. 'Hello?'

'Drew?'

'Shelley?' Did she imagine the wary note which had crept into his voice? 'What's happened?'

At least he had the sense to know that she would only be calling him in an emergency. 'Jennie's gone out with Jamie and I'm looking after Ellie, only she's sick—'

'Sick?' He fired out the question rapidly and she could hear someone in the background talking to him. 'How sick?'

'I don't *know*! She's vomited all over me, and I don't know whether it's just an upset stomach, or whether—'

'Stay right there!' he barked. 'I'm on my way over!'

She wasn't going anywhere! She hugged the baby to her with sheer relief. Because of all the men in all the world who she would choose to cope with any kind of emergency she knew exactly who would be her number one choice. 'Drew's coming,' she whispered against Ellie's clammy cheek.

She calculated that it would take him ten minutes at the earliest to scramble up the pebbly beach and into his car, and to drive over here.

He made it in five, letting himself in with his own key to find Shelley standing white-faced in the middle of the sitting room while Ellie continued to cry fretfully against her shoulder.

He ran his eyes over the two of them, before swiftly crossing the room to put the back of his hand over Ellie's forehead. 'How is she?' He scowled as he touched the baby's skin. 'Hell! The child's burning up!' he exclaimed urgently.

'What do we do?'

'We need to cool her down,' he said. 'Strip her off and put her on a towel first—I'll go upstairs and run a tepid bath.'

Shelley's hands were shaking as she struggled to get the vest over the child's head. She could hear Drew moving around upstairs and could have wept with relief when he came back down.

'We mustn't panic,' he said calmly as he took the naked child from her and cradled her in his arms.

'No. We mustn't.' Kind of him to say 'we' when he clearly meant 'you'. He seemed so cool-headed, acting as if he was used to dealing with an emergency like this every day of his life.

'Do you know where Jennie's gone?'

Shelley licked her lips nervously as she tried to remember. 'I think she said she was going to the Smugglers first—yes, I'm sure she did, but she mentioned going dancing, too!'

'Damn!' he swore. 'That means they've probably driven into Southchester.' He frowned and then nodded, as though he had made his mind up about something. 'Can you go and put Ellie in the bath? It's already run. Just lower her in slowly and dabble the water over her, so that her skin gets cooler. I'm going to ring for the doctor. Even if it is a false alarm.'

Shelley nodded. 'Yes, do.' She thought of Dr Milne who had seen her through every childhood ailment in the book. He didn't just know his stuff—he made you feel *safe*, too.

She carried Ellie upstairs and put her in the bath, remembering from something she'd read that you could lose a lot of heat through the surface of the head. She splashed some water over the baby's flushed face and Ellie kicked her legs, though whether it was in appreciation or in protest Shelley couldn't tell.

She heard someone coming up the stairs and suddenly there was Drew standing by the open door of the bathroom, too dark and too tall to do anything other than completely dominate the small room.

He looked down at the baby, and his face softened with concern. 'How is she?'

'The water seems to have quietened her down. Maybe we called the doctor too hastily?'

He shook his head. 'I don't care! Imagine if it was—' He seemed to swallow one word down and substitute another. '*Your* baby. Or mine.'

'Yes,' she said, trying to imagine Drew's baby. A baby he might very well have some day. *With somebody else.* Shelley was horrified to feel jealousy ripping through her like a sharp knife. 'I expect you're right.'

His eyes were trained on her. 'You're covered in baby-sick,' he observed. 'Do you want to—?' He paused delicately, and Shelley found it ironic that the presence of the baby seemed to have turned him into some kind of gallant. And as unlike the man who had made all kind of crude suggestions to her last week as was possible to imagine. 'Take something off?'

Shelley carried on calmly splashing the baby. At least that kept her occupied. 'It's only my sweatshirt. I'll wait until the doctor arrives—'

But then their eyes *did* meet as if some outside force

had compelled them to, and she dared him, just *dared* him to make some cheap crack about taking her clothes off at a time like this.

But he didn't.

'Okay,' he agreed. 'He should be here any minute. I'll go downstairs and phone the pub to see if Jennie is still there.'

A few minutes later she heard the front door open and close and Drew called up to her.

'Shelley? Can you bring her down?'

She wrapped the baby loosely in a big towel and carried her downstairs, startled when she saw that it wasn't the familiar family doctor who stood next to Drew at all, but a distinctly good-looking man of about forty who was just drying his hands.

His eyes flickered over Shelley with interest as she put the towel and the baby down on the floor of the sitting room, and he rolled his sleeves up to examine her.

He poked and prodded and gave a little grunt as he listened to Ellie's chest through his stethoscope.

'How is she?' asked Shelley and Drew at exactly the same moment and the doctor smiled.

'I can't hear anything on her chest. It's just a temperature at the moment—we'll have to keep an eye on her to check that she doesn't develop anything else—like spots or a rash. In the meantime, I'll give you something which will bring her temperature down.' He began taking something from his bag. 'If you turned the central heating down, it would help. And try to get as much clear, sweet fluid into her as you can. Hopefully, it will all blow over by the morning.' He looked at Drew. 'But tell Jennie to call me at any time if she's worried. I don't care if it's the middle of the night. Understand?'

'Okay. I will.' Drew nodded. 'Thanks, Jack.'

'Don't mention it.' The doctor glanced at Shelley and his eyes crinkled. 'Who are you, then? I'm Jack Simpson.'

'Shelley Turner,' she smiled. 'I'm pleased to meet you, Jack!'

'Oh, so *you're* Shelley!' Jack nodded, his eyes twinkling. He looked from Drew to Shelley as he stood up and picked up his bag. 'Maybe I should get my wife to invite you both over to dinner?'

Or maybe not, thought Shelley, watching Drew shrug his shoulders with a wry smile.

'I'm here out of necessity, Jack,' he murmured. 'Shelley and I weren't actually spending a cosy evening babysitting together.'

'Oh, I see.'

Once Jack had gone she felt...redundant...ill at ease. And not just because her top was all sticky. With the doctor there, the room had seemed a little crowded to start removing her clothes. But now he had gone—and she only needed to take her sweatshirt off. It wasn't as if she was about to strip down to lace panties and bra— for heaven's sake!

She quickly peeled the top off and wrinkled up her nose. 'Ugh!' she said, and ran upstairs to put it in the laundry. But when she came slowly back downstairs it was to find his eyes fixed on every step she took. 'That's better,' she said awkwardly.

'You look...*cooler*,' he commented, but his voice was husky.

Never had a simple white T-shirt felt more indecent. She felt it moulding itself to the contours of her body, outlining the sudden thrusting swell of her breasts. The small room felt even more crowded and even Drew had started to look distinctly agitated. 'Let's give Ellie this medicine,' he said roughly.

Shelley spooned the sticky mixture into the baby's mouth while Drew held her.

'Good girl,' he whispered to the baby.

Shelley held up one of the sachets which Jack had given them. 'I'll go and mix this up in a bottle for her.'

'Good girl,' he said absently.

'Are you talking to me this time, or talking to Ellie?'

He looked up and smiled. 'Sorry. But "good woman" doesn't have quite the same ring to it.'

Yes, it does, thought Shelley fiercely as she sterilised one of Ellie's bottles. Oh, yes, it does!

The baby glugged contentedly on Drew's knee and gradually she dozed off in his arms.

'Want me to take her?' she whispered, but he shook his head with a smile.

'I'm happy like this.'

'How about some coffee?'

He gave a murmur of approval. 'Kitten—you're a mind-reader!'

She wished she was! Then she might have some idea what was going on in that head of his. She went out into the kitchen and hunted around. 'I can only find instant!' she called back, after a minute.

'Instant's fine!'

She stuck her head round the door. 'Are you hungry?'

Drew made himself stare at her face, deliberately keeping his gaze as far from those amazing breasts as possible. He thought he'd rather have her in the dirty sweatshirt than in that outrageous white T-shirt. He had been just about to eat supper when she'd rung, but suddenly his appetite had deserted him.

'No,' he answered shortly, in case his voice betrayed him.

'Okay,' she shrugged.

She made the coffee and brought crackers and cheese in with it, noticing his eyes light up. Funny, she'd *known* he was hungry!

'I'll take her for a bit,' she said softly. 'Put her in my arms and try not to wake her.'

'What about your coffee?'

'It can wait.'

He carried the child over with infinite care and placed her in the waiting cradle of Shelley's arms. Ellie barely stirred, just wriggled her body luxuriously and sighed.

Drew picked up his coffee. 'Nice life being a baby,' he observed, glancing over at the contented picture they made.

'Easy,' she agreed.

There was a pause.

He sliced some cheese off the wedge. 'And how would you describe your life in Italy?' he found himself asking. 'Was that easy?'

She smiled, recognising the truce for what it was. You couldn't really continue waging a battle when you had a dependent little baby in your care. 'It's a myth that life is radically different in another country,' she mused. 'You still eat, sleep and go shopping just the same. Of course, the climate there is wonderful—and so is the food—but I wouldn't say that life was necessarily easier. Just different. I saw a lot of lovely things, had some fantastic experiences—like you must have done when you went travelling.'

'You must miss it,' he observed, wondering how much she missed *him*. Marco.

Shelley hesitated and he must have seen it, because he

said, 'Don't worry—I won't storm out of here feeling wounded on behalf of myself and everyone else in Milmouth if you tell me that yes, you miss it madly!'

'But I don't! I miss it much less than I imagined I would,' she told him, watching the strong hands as they cupped his mug of coffee. She wondered—hoped—that he wouldn't ask her about Marco. Not now. For wouldn't it spoil this strange feeling of contentment which had stolen over her? And Drew felt it, too—she could tell that from the way he had relaxed back into the chair, his face thoughtful as he drank his coffee.

He saw her watching. 'Quite like old times,' he observed.

She glanced down at the sleeping baby on her lap. 'Well, not quite!'

'No.' His smile was rueful. 'I guess not.'

It certainly had some of the ease of old times, but with an edge of uncertainty which added an unmistakable tension to the atmosphere. Shelley kissed the baby's head, thinking what a bizarre little trio they would make to someone who didn't know the true situation. Why, to an outside observer, they could almost be a family unit. If only she had gone with the flow of things, this *could* be them—only Ellie could be *their* baby. It was almost too poignant to bear.

'Do you want to go?' she asked him suddenly. 'It's late. Jennie said they might not get back until one.'

'No.' He shook his head and frowned. 'You go. I'll stay.'

'But Jennie will be expecting *me*, won't she?'

'She'll be expecting a responsible, caring adult and I think we both fit that category, don't you?'

'Why, thank you, Drew!' she murmured.

'Anyway, I'm staying,' he put in obstinately. 'I'm her

uncle and I'm perfectly capable of looking after her. What you do is up to you.' He narrowed his eyes and shot her a look of deepest blue. 'But you look dead beat, Shelley. Why don't you go to...?' A pulse flickered at his temple as he seemed to have trouble getting the word out without making it sound like an invitation. As he'd done in the restaurant. 'Bed...' he finished, wondering why certain words could sound so *explicit*. He stared at Shelley. It depended on who you said them to, of course.

'Maybe I will,' she said, hoping that if he noticed the pinkness of her cheeks he would put it down to the central heating. Except that they'd turned it right down...

'Of course—' his voice deepened '—you could always stay here and keep me company?'

As if! She remembered the sleepiness in his voice when he'd answered the phone, the voice in the background. She knew she had no right at all to ask and that asking might make her appear vulnerable, but her need to know overrode everything right then, including her judgement.

'Won't anyone be expecting you back home?'

'What makes you ask that?'

There seemed little point in beating around the bush. 'Because I heard someone speaking to you when I telephoned.'

'So you did.' He gave her a shrewd stare. 'And you want to know who it was, is that it? Whether somebody is keeping my bed warm for me, back home?'

'That wasn't what I asked you, Drew.'

'Liar!' The glitter in his eyes intensified. 'Not in so many words, maybe—but that was the point behind your question. You wanted to know if I was with a woman.' His voice was husky. 'And the answer is yes, I was.'

She felt the blood drain from her face and wondered

if it showed. She stood up carefully and carried the baby over to him, but at least it distracted her from the thump of pain she felt at the thought of somebody—*anybody*—in his bed. Bar her.

'Oh, I see.'

'Do you?'

'Perfectly.' She swallowed. 'And it's time I was going.'

His blue eyes were fixed unwaveringly on her face, wishing that she'd come straight out and ask him. Except that he still hadn't asked *her* about the Italian. Had he? 'Her name is Amanda and she's a friend.'

'A friend?'

'Sure. I have lots of friends of the opposite sex—don't you? Want to meet her?' he questioned. 'You could wait until Jennie gets back and I'll take you home with me.'

'I think I'll pass.'

'Another time, maybe?'

'We'll see.' Because she wasn't sure what part he was suggesting she play in his life—as another friend of the opposite sex, perhaps? And it wasn't the kind of question you could come straight out and ask a man. Even a man you'd once been engaged to—no, *especially* a man you'd once been engaged to.

She picked up her keys and both he and the baby looked up at her as they started to jangle like Christmas bells. 'I'm sorry if I disturbed your evening,' she said stiffly.

He smiled, but it was an empty smile. 'That's probably the most insincere thing you've ever said to me, kitten,' came the soft reply.

CHAPTER NINE

JENNIE came round the following morning to inform Shelley that Ellie had been suffering from a twelve-hour bug which she had quickly shrugged off in the way that only babies and children could.

'So she's okay?' asked Shelley.

'She's fine.' Jennie's eyes were like saucers. 'I couldn't believe it when I came back to find *Drew* there!' She pulled a face. 'Jamie wasn't very happy about it.'

'I wasn't ecstatic about it myself,' said Shelley. 'We don't have the easiest relationship in the world, as you know—but he was the first person I thought of calling when I saw she wasn't well.' She sighed. 'I have to say, though, that he was absolutely *brilliant*—though I sort of knew he would be!'

Jennie smiled. 'Funny—that's exactly what he said about you!'

'*Did* he?' Shelley clamped down her enthusiasm. 'What time did you get back?'

Jennie looked slightly sheepish. 'Er—about two.'

'And didn't Drew mind?'

'Well, he had a bit of a moan—but it was more on the lines of whether I had told *you* that I was going to be so late. And of course I hadn't. Sorry about that, Shelley.'

'Honestly—it doesn't matter.' She hesitated. 'How *was* your evening?'

'It was blissful—really blissful. And if Jamie weren't so worried about money all the time it would have been quite perfect.'

Shelley nodded but wondered just how realistic Jennie was being. It was all very well thinking that an injection of cash would make everything in her world wonderful, but life wasn't as simple as that. Wasn't that a bit like someone thinking that losing weight would solve every problem they had?

She broke into Jennie's distracted air with a question. 'How much does he actually need to buy the boat?'

Jennie shrugged and mentioned an amount which didn't seem particularly vast—not to Shelley, anyway. But then she was used to Marco's world, where enormous sums were made as profit on a single painting.

'And has he spoken to his bank manager?'

Jennie gave a cynical laugh. 'Oh, he's spoken to him, all right—but banks only seem to lend money to people who are already earning huge amounts of it—which makes you wonder why they want to borrow it in the first place!'

'Well, that's *one* way of looking at it, I suppose.'

She set about giving the house a proper face-lift, and hired a steamer to take off all the wallpaper in the hall then painted it bright blue. The modern walls were in good enough condition to take such a vivid colour and Shelley bought a huge mirror and hung it next to the door—so that the smallish space looked twice the size. She found a deep blue vase to stand on the floor and filled it with tall twigs which looked dramatic against the intense colour.

Decorating was hard work, but it meant that she slept well at night, after an indulgent evening of reading or television, with supper on a tray. Early each morning she would walk along the pebbly beach—sometimes taking

Ellie with her. It had always been her favourite time of day, when the sky and the sea were both at their purest.

But she resisted the urge to follow the small track down through the sand-dunes to take another look at the coastguard's cottage, even though she was tempted. She didn't want to be seen hanging around Drew's place like a groupie!

And there was no doubt in her mind that she felt a little *cheated*. After the definite truce which had sprung up when they'd looked after Ellie, he had dropped out of sight almost completely, and she found she missed him more than she wanted to. In fact, she saw him only once—standing windswept in front of one of the large seafront villas which she presumed he was working on. He was wearing jeans and a waterproof jacket and stood talking animatedly to another man, his dark head bent over some flapping sheets of paper which looked like plans.

She briefly toyed with the idea of asking Jennie just how good a friend Amanda was to Drew, but decided against it. Because it was none of her business. Was it?

And then one morning—out of the blue—he sent her an invitation to a fireworks party.

She recognised the writing on the envelope immediately—even though she hadn't seen it for years. He had a distinctive black-inked and crabbed style, and her heart was bashing out a very irregular rhythm as she ripped the envelope open.

'Bring any spare wood for the bonfire,' he had written at the top of the card.

It gave her a bit of a jolt to see that he was sending out proper *invitations*—but then maybe it really was time that she banished her image of the old Drew for ever. He now wheeled and dealed and part-owned hotels. He was a man comfortable in his own skin, and in his place within the community. *She* was the one still cast adrift.

She read down to the bottom of the card, where it said, 'Don't bother to reply since it's very casual. Just turn up if you feel like it.'

Which was extremely irritating because it meant that she didn't have to make a decision until the last possible moment! Anyway, she definitely wasn't going. Not unless Jennie was.

'No, I'm not going,' shrugged Jennie. 'I haven't been invited.'

'Oh. Don't you mind?'

'Not at all. I'm his sister, not his best buddy! Anyway, I wouldn't go without Jamie and there's no chance of Drew inviting him. Not unless he *changes his ways*, as my dear brother keeps saying,' said Jennie darkly. 'What Drew doesn't seem to realise is that Jamie's free spirit is the man I fell in love with—not some boring *suit* who works from nine to five!'

Shelley thought fleetingly that maybe there was something in between a free spirit and a boring suit—who could accommodate family life a little better than Jamie was currently doing! But she also thought that Drew was an unforgiving man. Did he really think that alienating Jamie would make him treat his sister better—or didn't he care?

She changed her mind at least fifty times about going, and then changed it back again. Maybe she would just stroll along and have a look. She looked in the mirror and scowled at her reflection.

She wasn't just having a bad-hair day—more like a bad-hair *month*! The trouble with a short, severely cropped style was that it looked awful when it started to grow out. As growing out it was—*fast*! She certainly wasn't going to keep having it cut and tinted every six weeks. What had seemed like the only thing to do in Milan now seemed like sheer madness here in Milmouth. She would rather walk on a windswept beach than sit with a plastic cape tied round her!

The highlights and lowlights were on their way out—leaving behind the caramel gloss which was her natural colour. And leaving her *roots*!

No, she definitely *wasn't* going!

And even if she was—she had nothing to wear. Nothing which was suitable for a beach party where everyone would be dressed down. She couldn't wear her blue jeans again because Drew would be bound to look at them and associate them with Ellie being sick all over her!

On the evening of November the fifth she was finger-drying her hair and telling herself that she would just wander down as far as the cottage to have a peep. And if it looked boring—unlikely—or, worse, if Drew had a woman draped all over him—much more likely—well, then she would quietly slip away and come home and drink a very large gin and tonic and put it all down to experience.

She wore her black jeans and the black cashmere sweater, though neither seemed quite as baggy as they had done when she'd first arrived.

Had she put on weight? She turned and looked criti-cally at her reflection. Maybe just a bit. Her bottom seemed more curved and her breasts a little heavier. She squinted. And if she was being objective rather than vain she had to admit that she didn't look too bad. She looked over her shoulder at her denim-clad rear. Not bad at all.

It was a perfect night for fireworks—pitch-dark, cold and clear, the sky thick with stars. Carrying a bottle of wine, a bag full of bits of old wood and a packet of sparklers, Shelley wrapped up warmly in a sheepskin jacket and let herself out into the starry night.

As she walked towards the beach she could hear the whizz and bang of fireworks, and over on the Isle of Wight she could just make out the ghostly red glow of a distant bonfire.

She passed the Smugglers, to see that the place was heaving. Although it was a bitter night, they had flung open the doors and people were already spilling out onto the green. They cradled drinks in their gloved hands while they waited for the arrival of the pyrotechnician to put on the traditional firework display.

Shelley made her way through the sand-dunes towards the cottage, and could tell immediately from the chatter of party voices that everyone was congregated outside in the garden—where large torches were flaming at various vantage points.

She approached in silence, and when she saw all the shadowed figures silhouetted against the spiky mountain of the bonfire she almost turned back. But maybe Drew had been looking out for her, or maybe it was just co-incidence that she heard his voice carry across the garden as he called her name.

'Shelley!'

She wished he hadn't. There were about twenty people milling around the place and they all looked round at once.

He came over and smiled down at her. 'Hi.'

'Hi.'

'Nice of you to come.'

'Nice of you to ask me.'

'My, aren't we being polite?' He raised his eyebrows. 'We *are* making progress!'

'Don't speak too soon!' she warned. 'Normal warfare could be resumed at any time!' But her voice lacked any kind of conviction and he smiled again.

'I gather that not only is Ellie eating everything in sight but she's actually started crawling?'

'Yes, she's better,' said Shelley. 'I took her out for a walk in her pushchair this morning.'

'I know you did.'

'How?'

'I saw you.'

Her breath seemed to catch in her throat. 'Did you?'

'Uh-huh.'

'But I didn't see you!'

'I know you didn't. You were far too busy bending to pick up Ellie's teddy which she seemed hell-bent on hurling into the sea!'

She chuckled, and he looked surprised, but then she guessed it was a long time since he had heard her laugh quite so uninhibitedly. And suddenly she wanted more than anything to fling her arms round him in a great big hug, as she would any old friend from way back. She contented herself with studying him, instead.

He wore black jeans too, and a bright scarlet sweater. He saw her looking at it and raised his eyebrows. 'Like it?'

'Love it,' she said lightly. 'No one will miss you coming, that's for sure!'

He laughed. 'The host should always be clearly visible—that's the second rule of parties.'

Now who had taught him that? she wondered. 'And what's the first rule?'

'Oh, that's easy.' There was a pause before he said, very deliberately, 'Only invite people you like.'

She gave him a wry look. 'So you like me now, do you, Drew?'

His eyes were rueful. 'I always did, Shelley—it might have been easier if I didn't.'

'Oh,' she said faintly, going pink with pleasure but hoping that he wouldn't notice in the dark. This was *crazy*! All their history and she was stricken with shyness—worse than anything she'd experienced the first time around! She held out the bag towards him.

'What's this?' he asked, taking it.

'These are the wooden remains of a wall cupboard I demolished when I was decorating.'

'Not the one in the hall?'

'That's the one! I hated it, I'm afraid.'

'No, I never liked it, either.'

Oh, the danger—the lazy and seductive danger of a shared past! Shelley quickly handed over the bottle. 'And here's some wine. I—' She had been about to say that she hoped he liked red, when she remembered that he did. 'Hope you like it.'

'Thank you.'

'And sparklers.'

'Why, thank you, Shelley,' he said gravely. 'Your hair looks good, by the way.'

She shook it in denial. 'It's all over the place. It needs a cut.'

'No, it doesn't. I prefer it longer.'

Suddenly she found that she wanted to grow it down to her bottom!

'Now come and get a drink and I'll introduce you to anybody you don't know.'

'I won't know anyone!' she groaned.

'Rubbish! You've met Jack, the doctor—he's here with

his wife. And Charlie from the shop. Plus, there are a couple of people you were at school with—'

She felt as though her nervousness would swallow her up. Maybe that was what made her drop her mask. 'Drew, these people are your friends. They'll hate me, resent me—'

'What for?' he asked, in surprise.

'For running away the way I did—'

'No, they won't.'

'I remember what it was like.'

'And it's ancient history, Shelley. People have moved on. Most people won't even remember.'

'And if they do?'

He shook his head. 'It's between you and me, kitten. Nobody else.'

She shivered, and it had nothing to do with the night air.

'Or would you rather look round and see what I've done to the cottage?' he asked suddenly.

Her heart crashed against her ribcage. 'No—' That sounded all wrong somehow. Slipping away with him when she'd only just arrived. 'Not yet.'

'What will you drink?'

'Anything.'

'Decisive kind of woman, are you?' he teased.

He had said that they were flirting that night at the Westward, but he had been wrong. They had made the same kind of noises as flirting, but there had been anger and bitterness distorting everything they said. Yet now each word they spoke seemed to be charged with about a hundred different allusions. *This* was flirting! *Really* flirting—and suddenly she didn't care. She held his gaze. 'I'll leave you to make your own mind up about that!'

Only a pulse beating furiously at his temple betrayed

the fact that he obviously wasn't feeling as calm as he looked. 'Right.'

A voice broke into the tension and shattered it.

'Come on, Drew—stop monopolising this beautiful woman and get round and fill everyone's glasses up— you *are* the host, man!'

It was Jack Simpson, who gave Shelley his crinkly smile. He was accompanied by a heavily pregnant woman with shiny hair, who was clinging onto his arm as if for support. Which, come to think of it, thought Shelley, she probably was.

'Go away,' growled Drew. 'Can't you see you're interrupting?'

'I'm paying you back for interrupting *me* the other night!' teased Jack.

'But that was work!' protested Drew, giving Shelley the helpless shrug of someone who knew they were beaten.

'So is this! When you throw a party you can't just chat up the women!' said Jack sternly. 'Or woman,' he amended, winking at Shelley. 'Someone was asking how the sound system works and I told them I didn't have a clue. Drag yourself away!'

Drew forced a smile. 'Right.' But still he didn't move. 'I'll get someone to bring you a drink over, Shelley.'

'Thanks.' Shelley watched him go, her heart aching more than her body because she knew now that she wanted him very badly. And not just his body—though she couldn't deny she wanted *that*. But she wanted his soul and his mind, too. His wit and his imagination. She wanted every little bit of him...

Was it too late? she wondered. Not to start *again* necessarily, but maybe to start anew...

Jack had placed a protective hand in the small of his

wife's back. 'Shelley, this is Rebecca—my ripe and beautiful spouse. Rebecca, meet Shelley Turner. Remember I told you about her?'

Rebecca smiled. 'Oh, *you're* Jennie's friend.'

'Yes, I am.' Shelley smiled back. 'Your husband was absolutely brilliant the other night when I was babysitting for Ellie. She's fine now,' she added.

'Yes, I know,' said Jack. 'I popped in the next morning on my way back from surgery to find her howling with hunger!' He sniffed the air. 'Mmm! Are those sausages I smell?'

'That's all you ever think about!' teased his wife, but he looked meaningfully at her swollen belly and murmured, 'Oh, *really*?'

Shelley was wondering where her drink was when a tall woman who was dressed, like her, entirely in black came across the garden towards them. She was carrying a steaming glass of what smelt like gluhwein in one hand, and a bowl of cashew nuts in the other.

'Hi, Rebecca! Hi, Jack!' Air kisses all round. She turned to Shelley. 'Hello, there—I know you're Shelley but you don't know me! *Yet*!' she giggled. 'I'm Amanda! Drew told me to fetch you a drink, and so—like his ever-faithful slave—here I am! And here *you* are!'

Willing her fingers not to shake, Shelley stretched her hand out and took the steaming punch-glass from her. 'Thank you.'

Shelley took a sip of her drink which meant she could get a good look at Amanda without appearing to stare too much. Close up, she could see that her dark hair was in a shiny French plait all the way down her back. She looked ultrafeminine and vibrant, and Shelley suddenly felt shorn and vulnerable with her neck all bare and her ears showing.

Rebecca turned her face up to her husband. 'Darling, can we go and find me a seat somewhere?' she asked him plaintively.

Jack smiled, and bent to kiss the tip of her nose. 'Oh, you're going to milk this pregnancy for all you're worth, aren't you, my love? Have me running round in circles after you!'

Rebecca's smile was serene and dreamy. 'Of course I am! What do you expect the fifth time round?' She shot him a look from beneath her lashes. 'You'll just have to stop getting me pregnant, Jack Simpson!'

'Only if you stop making yourself so irresistible!'

'*Jack!*'

Jack winked at Shelley and Amanda. 'Excuse us, please, ladies!' And he decorously led his wife across the lawn towards the house.

'*Five?*' queried Shelley, aghast.

'I know. It's unbelievable, isn't it?' asked Amanda as they watched them go. 'That beautiful, serene-looking woman has four at home and another on the way—whatever it is she's taking, *I* want some of it!'

The slap of the waves against the shore from the nearby beach was hypnotic, and Shelley's attention was caught by the sight of Drew adding a couple of pieces of wood to the unlit bonfire. She watched him while pretending not to, as up above them the stars dazzled their pale fire over the indigo sky.

'Gorgeous, isn't it?' asked Amanda, looking around. 'I love this setting. Drew has the best house in Milmouth, in my opinion. I said to him the other night, If you're ever thinking about selling up, then I want first option!'

'Have you known him…very long?'

'Only about a year. Charlie and I met him when we took over the shop.'

Shelley frowned as Amanda's words clicked into place. 'Charlie's your husband?'

Amanda looked slightly nonplussed. 'Yes, of course he is! I thought you knew that. We were having drinks with Drew the other night when you telephoned to say that Ellie was sick. I was offering to go with him as my baby is the same age as Ellie. I thought he told you?'

'Yes, he did,' agreed Shelley slowly. 'He told me you were there.' But he had omitted to tell her that Charlie had been there, too. Or that Amanda had a husband. He had just answered her question honestly, so that she had been able to put two and two together and come up with a number somewhere in the thousands! Now why had he done that?

'Look!' said Amanda suddenly, and they saw Drew put a light to the base of the bonfire, and watched the slow orange sparking as the fire began to crackle.

The smell of smoke mingled with the smell of the sea while the sound of chattering voices competed with the rush of the waves, and as Shelley let her guard down she began to relax more than she had done for ages. 'See how quickly the fire has taken,' she murmured, watching as tongues of flame began to lick at the wood.

'Do you want to come and meet some people?' smiled Amanda. 'Drew said to make sure you had a good time because hosts get tied up!'

'Not literally, I hope!' Shelley quipped as a rather disturbing image popped into her mind. Of Drew bound helplessly by hand and foot...

She looked over to where he stood by the bonfire, his head bent as he listened to what a tiny woman in a microskirt was saying to him. Shelley took a hasty mouthful of punch and looked away. She'd leapt to all the wrong conclusions about Amanda—so maybe it was time she gave up on that kind of thing. 'Yes, I'd love to come and meet some people, Amanda!'

She chatted to Charlie, who told her that word on the ground was that a clothes shop would be a very welcome addition to the village.

'So will you think about it?' he added.

'I'll *think* about it!' she promised.

She met a couple who had holidayed near Marco's villa and wanted to talk restaurants, then caught up with the two old schoolfriends Drew had mentioned. She hadn't seen Marianne and Nicola for years and both were married, with one expecting twins!

'Everyone here seems to be pregnant!' exclaimed Shelley.

'Must be something in the water!' Marianne surveyed her swollen stomach with a rueful expression. 'Remember that time we all sunbathed topless on the beach, Shelley?'

'*Do* I?'

'And Drew came over all furious and protective and masterful,' Nicola sighed.

Shelley nodded. 'That's right. He did. Some people might have said that he came on very heavy!' She knew what was coming next. A question on the lines of what exactly was happening between her and Drew nowadays. A question she did not want to answer, simply because she couldn't. She didn't know herself. Maybe nothing.

Maybe it was naive to suppose that, just because they were no longer hurling abuse at each other, something romantic was waiting to burst into life instead. The only thing she *was* sure of was that he still wanted her physically, only this time he was prepared to follow through. And this time she didn't even have the reassurance of knowing that he loved her. It was time to move away.

She raised her empty glass. 'I'm going to find another of these before the fireworks start,' she said.

'There'll be fireworks starting any minute now if my husband has much more to drink,' said Nicola grimly, her eyes fixed on a tall man at the other side of the garden who seemed to be having difficulty maintaining his balance.

Shelley looked around the garden for Drew but couldn't find him, so she wandered off towards the house to see just what he had done with it.

He had certainly kept it simple—but then, it had such a fabulous location that fussy decor would have taken attention away from the stunning views.

The kitchen was painted in a soft turquoise, with units in a deeper shade. There were windows on three sides of the room, and one which directly overlooked the sea. Now the water was as dark and glossy as oil, but she thought how wonderful it must look during the day— almost as if you could reach your hand out and touch the waves themselves.

She filled her glass and strolled down the corridor leading to the sitting room, where she could see a log smouldering in the grate of an enormous fireplace. She liked the kitchen. She liked it very much. She wondered what he had done to the sitting room.

The floor was made of bare boards and her deck shoes made no sound on the polished wood. She passed a set of exquisite mirrors, each one different, their frames encrusted with shells.

She only got a brief impression of what the interior of the room was like—sky-blue walls and a vast painting of a boat—because a noise from the far end of the room distracted her, and when she looked she could see a big, book-lined study.

But that wasn't the only thing she saw. Two figures stood engaged in deep conversation, one instantly recognisable and one not.

The recognisable one was male and tall and rangy with dark, honey-tipped hair, while the unrecognisable one was female, freckled and had an aggressively assertive tilt to her pelvis.

And of course, on closer inspection, she wasn't *completely* unrecognisable—because it was the woman who had been talking to Drew so animatedly by the bonfire, noticeable mainly for the length of her skirt. Or rather the lack of length. Shelley had thought that on a bitterly cold night it was a little pointless to wear a mini-skirt—especially when every other female in the place was in jeans.

But maybe it wasn't so pointless. If the point had been to attract Drew Glover, then it looked as though she had succeeded very well.

Shelley hunched her shoulders up as she shrank against the wall and watched them, like an animal retreating into the protection of its shell, and for one crazy moment she could have sworn that Drew saw her. But no, he was too wrapped up in what was happening in front of him to notice anything.

She saw the woman, or girl—for she looked virtually pre-pubescent in such a ridiculous outfit—reach her arms up around Drew's neck and push that assertive pelvis towards him.

He didn't push her away.

Like watching a silent movie, Shelley saw her laughingly say something before raising a moist, eager mouth to his…

Shelley wanted to scream from the base of her lungs, but she couldn't bear to add humiliation to her agony.

She slunk back along the corridor like a thief and put her glass down on the table with trembling hands. And once outside she was swallowed up by the darkness, unnoticed by the laughing faces collected round the now blazing bonfire.

Shelley knew the area like the back of her hand; she knew which paths were unobserved and which ones to take so that she would not be followed.

But who was she fooling? There was no sound of frantic footsteps. No hot pursuit on her heels. And why would there be? Drew was a free agent. He could do what the hell he liked. Just because she had started to imagine happy-ever-after or some kind of resurrection of their doomed affair, that didn't make *him* an active participant in her fantasies.

She waited until she was clear of the house before she started to run, and then the sky started to explode in a cascade of golden rain and a shower of silver stars which were brighter and more dazzling than the real thing.

Someone must have let the fireworks off.

She thought that the pub must have lit theirs at almost the same time as Drew, for there were far too many to be just from one source. She heard the gunfire sound of bangers and saw a breathtaking eruption of emerald and deep rose-pink against the backdrop of the sky, but mainly gold, always gold—so that the sky looked lit up in celebration.

Some celebration!

She ran nearly all the way home, only slowing down as she approached her house. She didn't want the sound of pounding footsteps to alarm Jennie.

But Jennie's curtains weren't drawn and Shelley could see her moving around the sitting room, bending down to pick up discarded toys and putting them unenthusiastically into a box.

Her whole body carried an air of defeat about it, as if life held no joy for her. And maybe that was exactly how she felt. She was in love with the father of her child who in turn was made to feel inadequate because he worked like a dog simply to break even. Even if Jamie *did* move in next door, he would still have to live with the galling knowledge that Drew was his disapproving landlord.

And Shelley suddenly discovered that it was easy to channel her feelings of hurt into those of righteous indignation. Because you would think that Drew—of *all* people—would sympathise with Jamie. Hadn't he once been in the same position himself?

Why wouldn't Drew give Jamie the financial help he needed to make something of himself? Not because he wasn't able to, that was for sure.

She had seen the boat and been convinced of its investment value. So had Gerald O'Rourke. She had watched Jamie hard at work, and heard the respect with which Gerald spoke about him. And old boatmen like Gerald didn't give their approval easily.

An idea grew in her mind with the speed of a weed pushing its way up towards the sun. It was so simple she wondered why she hadn't thought of it before. Why didn't *she* step in and help out? Why not use some of her savings to help Jennie and her partner—just for the sheer altruistic hell of it?

And if Drew objected?

Well, so what? She didn't have to follow the same rigid, controlling path in life that he was obviously hell-bent on!

She thought about the sum Jennie had mentioned. It

wasn't a fortune exactly, but it was still a lot of money. What would Marco have said? She unlocked her front door slowly. She didn't have to decide tonight.

She would sleep on it.

CHAPTER TEN

IT WAS midday when Shelley opened the front door in response to the furious ringing of the bell. 'Drew!' she exclaimed in surprise more than anything, and then, *'Drew!'* in confused alarm as he pushed his way past her, straight into the sitting room.

She calmly followed him in there because she had been half expecting such a visit. And whatever he wanted she was going to keep her dignity. If he told her that the kiss at the party last night had all been a mistake, she was going to shrug her shoulders and say that what he did was his business, and nothing to do with her.

Of course, the fact that it was now midday probably meant that it had been anything *but* a mistake. No doubt he had only just dragged himself from the Pelvis's bed. Those looked pretty dark shadows underneath his eyes...

She folded her arms across her chest and fixed him with a questioning look. 'Yes, Drew? And to what do I owe this charming entrance?'

He seemed to be having difficulty keeping his breathing under control. 'Did you or did you not,' he said, biting each word out carefully, 'lend Jamie a substantial sum of money early this morning?'

She frowned. 'That's my business—'

'No!' He cut across her words with deadly intent. 'No, no, *no*! That's just where you're wrong, kitten! It involves my sister, and therefore it involves me—and that makes it *my* business!'

'And? What if I did?'

168

'Well, then—' he sucked in a low breath '—I'd like to know exactly *what* you think you're playing at.'

The look of righteous fury which had darkened his face so that he resembled some kind of devil made her feel slightly uneasy. But not for long. She was *not* going to be intimidated by him.

'I'm not *playing* at anything!' she snapped. 'I knew what the financial situation was with Jennie and Jamie and I knew how unhelpful you had been—'

'What did you know?' he snarled.

'That you had refused to invest in a sure-fire scheme to make money! I've looked at the boat and I'm surprised at you, Drew—*you* more than anyone should know that a lucky break is all you need some time!'

He shook his head. 'But that's where you're completely wrong, kitten—I did it all myself! I didn't ask anybody to cushion my way with handouts—'

'Which is one of the reasons we split up, isn't it? Because you nearly killed yourself in the struggle to make yourself the man you are today! Only we didn't have a baby, did we, Drew?'

His mouth tugged into a grim line, but his voice sounded oddly restrained. 'No. We didn't.'

'And we didn't have anybody we could go and ask for money either!'

'And if we had, do you think I would have gone out—cap in hand—looking for capital?'

Shelley sighed. That was the trouble. No. She didn't. He was a stubborn, stubborn man! He had done it all on his own—but at what price?

'That's irrelevant!' She pushed away an irritating strand of newly grown hair which kept flopping into her eyes. 'I happened to have some spare cash which I wasn't using and I thought, Why not put it to some good use?

So I went down to the boatyard and saw the boat in question—I even spoke to Gerald O'Rourke who wouldn't stop praising Jamie's maritime qualities—and you know what an old cynic *he* is! The boat was a good price—Jamie can't lose on it.' She shrugged her shoulders. 'I can't understand what your problem is, Drew. I should have thought you would have been glad to make your sister happy!'

He shook his dark head angrily. 'What a naive and gullible little fool you are, Shelley! If that were the case, then why the hell do you think I didn't loan him the money myself?'

'Bloody-mindedness?' she challenged.

'You know, I feel sorely tempted to throw you over my knee and wallop the living daylights out of you—'

'You wouldn't dare!'

'No, you're right—I wouldn't!' He sucked in a breath. 'Don't you think I know my sister's partner a little better than you do after—what—three meetings?'

'I—'

'And the reason I've never loaned Jamie so much as a bar of soap is because he seems unable to do anything other than fritter it away—like a student determined to blow his grant in one evening! As he has demonstrated once again.'

Something in his voice was beginning to alarm her. 'Wh-what do you mean?'

'I'll tell you exactly what I mean! I mean that the boat is sitting in the boatyard in the same place as it was yesterday and the day before. And that Jamie seems to have disappeared with all the money you loaned him. No one's seen him—not his mother, not the boatyard and not, most importantly of all, Jennie and his daughter.'

'Oh, no,' she whispered.

'Oh, yes,' he contradicted darkly.

'So what do we do?'

'*We?*' he mocked. 'Shouldn't that be *I*? I should leave you to sort out the whole bloody mess you've created for yourself!'

'Go on, then!'

'Oh, no!' He shook his head. 'I'm going out to find him and I'm going to bring every single penny back. For Ellie's sake more than anything.' He scowled. 'Having a father in jail for obtaining money by deception is not what I'd call the best start in life. But I'll tell you another thing, Shelley Turner—'

She narrowed her eyes at him suspiciously, sensing trouble. 'What?'

'That I don't believe you were simply motivated by a need to help Jennie and Ellie. I don't think you're that good a person!'

'Oh, don't you?'

'Not right now, no! I happen to think that your action was driven by a need to strike out and hurt *me*—'

'*No!*'

'*Yes!*' he snarled. 'You knew that I was opposed to the loan, but you went right ahead with it anyway. As an act of revenge it was pretty spectacular!'

'And why would I want to do that?'

'Think about it, kitten,' he said, as he fished a gleaming shoal of car keys from the pocket of his jeans. 'Just think about it!'

Shelley would have plenty of time to think about it in the next twenty-four hours, but first she knew that she had to go next door to see Jennie.

Jennie was red-eyed from weeping.

'I'm so sorry,' breathed Shelley.

Jennie shook her head and sniffed. 'It's my fault,' she moaned. 'I made out that Drew was just being tight, when really it was more to do with the fact that I couldn't face up to Jamie's spendthrift ways. If only you'd *told* me what you were intending to do, Shelley!'

But she hadn't known herself—and if she admitted to impulse that would make it a hundred times worse. 'Jamie made… No, someone can't *make* you do anything,' she amended. 'He asked me not to tell you. Said he wanted to buy the boat and wrap a big ribbon round it for you. And he also said he wouldn't be able to keep it a secret for long. That's why I drew the money out in cash.'

'*Cash!*' echoed Jennie, going positively pea-green. 'Oh, my word! What if he's spent it all by the time Drew catches up with him?'

'*If* Drew catches up with him,' said Shelley grimly.

'Oh, he will. You can be very sure of that.'

'Well, in that case—' she swallowed down her guilt as she thought about how her stupidity and her stubbornness might have reduced her savings by a third '—I'll just have to put it down to experience.'

The hours ticked by with agonising slowness, but she didn't dare leave the house in case there was any news. She was unenthusiastically thinking about preparing herself some supper when the doorbell rang and she rose to her feet, hardly daring to hope.

Her heart leapt at the sight of the broad-shouldered shadow standing outside, but her face was cautious as she opened the door to him. He had been seething with rage earlier, and although he might have felt that his anger was justified she wasn't sure if she would care to repeat the experience.

She drew a deep breath. 'Hello, Drew,' she said quietly.

'Can I come in?'

'Of course you can come in.' She stepped aside, not daring to speak.

It wasn't until they were facing each other warily across her sitting room that she summoned up the courage to ask. 'Any news?'

'I've found him,' he said flatly.

'Oh, thank God! Is he okay?'

Drew shook his head in disbelief. 'The man walks away with a great stack of your cash, without any intention of using it for the specified purpose of the loan—and you ask me is he *okay*?'

'Someone could have robbed him and beaten him up!'

'Shelley!' he howled, and then, unexpectedly, he smiled. And kept smiling. 'Yes, he's okay! Fortunately, I caught up with him before he managed to work his way through more than a couple of hundred pounds of the money. He told me that he was planning to come back anyway—but he was drunk when he said that, so I don't know if it was true.'

'And where is he now?'

'At his mother's house,' said Drew grimly. 'Sobering up. Actually, can you pour me a drink?' he asked suddenly, and flopped down into an armchair. 'I think I need one.'

She didn't comment on the irony of his request, just poured him a gin and tonic which was all she had. He took a large swallow and winced, before putting the glass down and delving deep into the pocket of his jeans. Always a distracting movement, thought Shelley as she watched him, like a cat watching a mouse.

He withdrew a wad of banknotes and threw them down on the table. 'These are yours. The exact amount—'

'Minus two hundred,' she agreed.

'No,' he contradicted. 'Minus nothing. It's all there. I made up the amount myself—'

'Drew, I can't—'

'Shelley, you can, and believe me you're going to. Jamie is family—kind of—so he's partly my responsibility. And that's an end to it.'

'I don't deserve it,' she said, in a small voice.

'No, you probably don't,' he agreed, but at his mouth was another glimmer of a smile and she knew that she had to tell him the truth.

'You were right all along,' she sniffed.

'No crying, Shelley. I refuse to be manipulated by your tears,' he warned her softly, then frowned suspiciously. 'You mean about Jamie squandering money?'

She shook her head. 'No—about the reason I lent him the money in the first place! It's true—I did it as a spectacular act of revenge—to use your very own words!'

'I see.' He leaned his head back and his eyes were half-closed. 'And what was your reason for this spectacular act of revenge?' he asked calmly, as if it were the sort of question he asked every day.

'Because I saw you kissing that…that—' She swallowed down her first choice of word. Bitchiness was never an attractive quality. '*Woman* at your party.'

The eyes opened an interested fraction. 'And why on earth would that bother you, Shelley?'

She turned on him. 'Why do you think? Do you want me to spell it out for you?'

'Not really. I want you to say it out loud for me instead.'

Her eyes were very bright and very clear. 'That I love

you? That I've always loved you? Surely you must know that by now?'

He didn't answer at first, just eased himself out of the chair as though he found sitting down inhibiting, but the blue eyes were as cold as a winter sea. 'Then you fall in love very easily, don't you, Shelley? Last month Marco, this month me.'

She shook her head, knowing that she needed to tread very carefully here. 'But I never loved Marco.'

'No?' He gave a dry laugh. 'You just lived with him for three years? That's some kind of devotion!'

'Yes, it is, I agree—but it's not love.' Her eyes blazed out the truth at him. 'And it never was—it was never anybody but you.'

There was silence and Shelley stared down at her hands, unable to look him in the face.

'Then why didn't you come back sooner if that was the case? Why stay with a man you claim not to have loved?'

She knew that she had to have the courage to face him, but she almost flinched from the accusation in the burning blue gaze. 'Like when?'

'When your mother died.' His eyes asked a question. 'I thought you would have needed me then.'

'Needed you?' She shook her head in despair. 'Oh, Drew—of course I *needed* you! If you'd shown the slightest indication that you wanted or needed *me*—then I would have come back like a shot! But you wouldn't even speak to me—bar the absolute minimum that you needed to—so how could I tell you anything? I was waiting for you to say something, *anything* that would have given me the smallest hint that you still wanted me. But you didn't. Sometimes I used to dream that you would come to Italy to find me, but you never did.'

'Because you were living with another man!' he ground out incredulously. 'What the hell did you expect—that I would walk in and drag you from his arms? Sorry, kitten, but that's just not my style!'

She opened her mouth to answer, but found herself gazing helplessly at him instead. And the only thing which seemed to matter now was whether or not it was too late for them. 'Drew?' she managed eventually.

She read the look in his eyes which made her dare to hope, and then suddenly she was wrapped in his arms so tightly that she could barely breathe.

'And please don't ask me if I still love you,' he whispered harshly, 'when I never stopped! Though God knows it wasn't for want of trying!' And with that he brought his mouth crushing down on hers in a kiss that made her want to melt into him and never be prised apart.

It took some time for him to tear his mouth away, and when he did he cupped her face tenderly with his hands.

'As for that woman you saw me with at the party—'

'You don't have to justify anything to me.'

He carried on as if she hadn't spoken. 'I knew you were there,' he said softly.

Shelley stilled, still sensitive to the possibility of... *betrayal*? 'Y-you *saw* me?'

'Sure I did. I saw you watching her kiss me.'

'You kissed her back!' she accused.

'I was a passive participant,' he argued. 'Not an active one.'

'And you think that makes it all right?'

He shook his head. 'I didn't stop her—that was the extent of my involvement. But if you'd hung around you'd have discovered that I rejoined the party minutes later and wondered where you'd gone.'

'You must have known damned well where I'd gone! That I couldn't stay there seeing you with someone else!'

He nodded. 'Yes, I knew what you must be thinking. I knew your mind must have been working overtime, as mine once did when I saw you with Marco. Don't you realise, kitten, just how powerful the imagination can be? And how dangerous? That it can be both weapon and tool? That's what I wanted to show you. All those times you shrugged your pretty shoulders and said, "Oh, Drew—it was just a kiss!" It's never *just* a kiss! You've always thought that I completely overreacted all those years ago—but you're guilty of exactly the same reaction, Shelley!'

He was right. She looked up at him, slightly shamefaced. 'Yes,' she whispered. 'I stormed out and took all that money out of the bank! I didn't even *think* of Jamie, I'm ashamed to say. All I could think of was how much it would infuriate you!'

He nodded. 'Both kisses were innocent—logic tells us that—but logic doesn't have much of a role to play when it comes to love. Passion dominates logic.' He gave her a long, searching stare. 'And I think it's about time we gave passion a little room in our lives, don't you, kitten? It's been waiting for long enough to come in.'

She grazed a finger across the rough, dark shadow of his chin. 'You need a shave,' she whispered.

'I need more than a shave. I need you like I've never needed anything or anyone in my life before. But not here.' He gave a slow smile that made her cheeks glow pink, then looked around the room. 'I don't want to stay here.'

'Why not?'

'Too many…memories. Come on.' He took her hand and kissed it. 'Let's go home to bed.'

CHAPTER ELEVEN

THE moon rose high in a sky of flawless navy velvet and silver light flooded in through the uncurtained window, illuminating the rumpled sheets and the two tangled bodies which lay amidst them.

Drew listened to the subsiding beat of her heart before he moved away so that she was at arm's length. More importantly, so that he could see her.

'So why didn't you tell me, Shelley?'

She let her eyelids drift open and yawned. She wasn't going to pretend not to know what he was talking about. 'It's a difficult topic to bring up. I couldn't think of the right time.'

'You could have told me any time. Especially before I…before we…' Suddenly he couldn't wipe the stupid grin off his face '…made love.'

She propped herself up on one elbow and raised her flushed face to his with a sleepy smile. 'I didn't want to tell you then.'

'Why not?'

'Because it would have made too big a deal of it—'

'Hell, Shelley—*it* is a big deal—or rather it's supposed to be! Taking a woman's virginity is one of the biggest—' His mouth quirked when he saw her expression. 'Stop it, will you? I'm *trying* to be serious! Do you want to tell me…just tell me how you're still a virgin?'

'You know very well *how*,' she retorted. 'Because I never made love to a man before. I think you mean why.'

'Don't play word-games with me at a time like this, kitten!' he pleaded.

She thought of asking him which games he *did* want to play at a time like this, but something in the way he was looking at her made her realise how much it meant to him.

And to her.

'Marco was... No, let me start again... Marco is...'

'For heaven's sake, Shelley, don't keep me in suspense, just say it!'

'Gay.'

'Gay?'

'That's right. He isn't interested in women—he never has been. That stupid kiss in the car was a thank-you kiss which went on longer than it should have done. It was always more about my fantasy than his. We lived together like brother and sister, until eventually he fell in love.' She examined his face. 'Are you shocked?'

'Shocked?' He gave a slow, easy smile. '*Shocked?* Kitten, I'm ecstatic, if you want the truth.' He turned onto his back and looked up at the bare ceiling with the wonder of a man who was gazing on the interior of the Sistine Chapel. 'Ecstatic! More than ecstatic! Good old Marco!'

He turned over to face her again and placed a possessive hand on her hip and frowned. 'So what was in it for him?'

Shelley smiled. 'He was a gorgeous, attractive, eligible and *fabulously* rich man and he used to get so many come-ons, you wouldn't believe it. Well, maybe *you* would! But he was adamantly opposed to sex without love. I scared people away for him, if you like. Men *and* women. He always said he would find true love one day, and now he has.'

'And if he hadn't—how much longer would you have stayed there?'

Shelley shrugged, realising now the danger in her apathy. 'I kept putting off having to make a decision. This was the only place I wanted to come back to, but I knew how impossible it would be if you'd found someone else.'

'Well, I hadn't.' He sighed. 'A virgin! Shelley, sweetest—you still could have told me first—I would have been a damn sight more gentle with you.'

'But I didn't want you to be gentle with me,' she said demurely. 'And neither did I want you to know I was a virgin *before* we made love. I needed to know that you would still want me even if I *had* had a lover before. As you've had lovers—'

'Not as many as you seem to imagine. In fact, the actual number—'

But she shook her head. 'The number isn't important, Drew. What *is* important is that you treat me as your equal. If you'd known I was a virgin, I'd have been back up there on that pedestal—and it got kind of lonely up there.'

'And did I? Treat you equally?'

'You know you did,' she said softly.

'Well, then, now it's your turn to hear *me* out. And on the question of lovers—'

'Drew!' she warned. 'I don't want to hear!'

'Well, you're going to! I may have had affairs in my life, but there has been no one—' he saw her incredulous face as she anticipated his words '—I repeat, no one—not since you went away to Italy.'

'*What?*'

'It's true.' He gave a long, lazy smile as he stroked a fingertip along the curve of her waist. 'I was so busy building up the business that I used to just fall into bed every night—alone! But more than that—' he smiled at the question in her eyes '—the simple truth is that there was no one I fancied as much as you, kitten. Not before and certainly not since.'

But despite the wonder of his words a sudden rush of melancholy swamped her. 'Oh, Drew—when I think of how much time we've wasted.'

'No.' His blue gaze was very intense as he smoothed the damp hair back from her face. 'We mustn't look on it as time spent wasted, but time spent growing. Neither of us was ready. I shouldn't have teased you and tried to control you, not when you were ripe with need and in love with me. I shouldn't have tried to control the inevitable. To fight fate. Even though I told myself that my intentions were purely honourable.'

'And I shouldn't have been so impatient!'

The gaze which flickered over her moon-washed body was rueful. 'You were an awesome responsibility when you were younger, you know, Miss Turner. Your mother was terrified of history repeating itself.'

'Was that why you...why we...?'

He sighed. 'She trusted me to take care of you, and I didn't want to abuse that trust. She once asked me not to take advantage of the crush you had on me, you know.'

'Did she?'

'Uh-huh. It was just after I'd caught you topless on the beach and I think she suspected that *my* feelings might have changed. And she was right of course. I wanted you so badly that it hurt. But I was going away, so I thought I'd forget all about you. You were almost eighteen and I was twenty-five, and so I rather arrogantly gave her my word that I wouldn't compromise you. And having given my word, kitten, how could I then break it?'

'Thank you,' she said simply, recognising only now the debt she owed him for his decency and his dependability.

'Then, when the whole understandable Marco thing happened, I was too arrogant and too proud to listen to reason. Arrogant for letting you go in the first place, and too proud to ask you to come back. Your mother always said you would, you know.'

'But you didn't believe her?'

'A part of me wanted to,' he sighed. 'But my pride stood in the way. I convinced myself that I couldn't care less. How about that for self-delusion?' He leaned across and brushed his lips against hers and she shivered with pleasure, trickling her fingers down the hair-roughened torso—from neck to belly button. 'We've waited one hell of a long time for this!' he growled.

'I know. But what we just shared was—' She couldn't think of a word which would say it all. 'For years we've had this slow, drugging build-up of the senses, and to-day...' She sighed with memory. 'Oh, Drew—wasn't it worth waiting for?'

'It was more than that, kitten.' He moved closer. 'It was the best thing that's ever happened to me,' he told her simply. 'Want to make it happen again? Right now?'

She wrapped her arms around his neck. 'Oh, yes, please,' she whispered. 'And now there are no secrets left between us, no barriers left to fall—'

'It's the final seduction?' He smiled with delight as he slowly lowered his head. 'Heart, body and soul...'

'You've got it,' she murmured, opening her lips to greet his. 'You've got it in one!' But her words were muffled against the sweetness of his kiss.

*   *   *

They spent the next twenty-four hours in bed and Shelley guessed that they must have slept at some point, only she wasn't exactly sure when.

They were sitting facing one another in the bathtub and Drew was showing her how very erotic a toe could be when she plucked up the courage to ask, 'What's going to happen with Jamie and Jennie?'

He scowled. 'I told Jamie that if he ever hurt my sister he would live to regret it. And that I was giving him a chance to make good.' He saw the look of bewilderment on Shelley's face. 'I've loaned him the money myself to buy the boat. The rest is up to him.' His eyes glittered dangerously. 'He'd just better not blow it. That's all.'

She leaned across the bubbles and kissed his nose tenderly. 'You're a bit of a pussy-cat when it boils down to it, aren't you, Drew Glover? Lending him all that…all that…' Her eyes widened in horror as she remembered. '*Drew!* All that money! We've left all that money lying on the table in the sitting room! Anyone could have broken in and stolen it!'

'Come on!' He climbed out of the bath and lifted her out. Then he threw over her discarded jeans and a thick navy sweater of his. 'Put this on!'

Despite the fact that she might have lost a great deal of money, she couldn't help smiling as she wriggled it over her head. Because it smelt of him—and now she felt as though he had filled every one of her senses. They jumped into his car and drove as fast as was safe and when they let themselves breathlessly into Shelley's house they discovered that the money had indeed disappeared from the coffee table.

'It's gone!' said Shelley dully.

'Well, it would be, wouldn't it? We might as well have posted a bloody great notice on the outside of the house.

Of all the stupid things to do!' But his eyes were soft. 'I guess the only defence we can offer is that we had other things on our mind.'

'Mmm.' She reached up on tiptoe to kiss him, because—rightly or wrongly—the money didn't seem to matter a bit right then. She had far more important things to think about. Like love. 'We certainly did!'

'We'll have to report it,' he sighed.

'Maybe there are fingerprints,' said Shelley hopefully.

'Better not touch anything!' He looked around and frowned. 'I wonder how the hell they got in? There's no sign of a break-in. You'd better see if they've taken anything else, kitten.'

Just then the front doorbell chimed and when Shelley went to answer it she found Jennie and Jamie standing on the doorstep. Jamie was holding Ellie and looking terribly pleased with himself while Jennie looked as though she was just bursting to tell them something.

'What are you doing here?' Drew asked suspiciously.

'Have you lost something?' asked Jamie airily.

'Like…?'

'Like this stash of cash?' questioned Jamie triumphantly, bringing his spare hand from behind his back and waving the wad of cash in the air.

'Where the hell did you get that?'

'Jamie saw it sitting on your table!' said Jennie, taking it from Jamie and handing it over to Shelley. 'And came and told me. We decided that it was too risky to leave it there. So we let ourselves in with the spare key you gave me, and took it home to keep it safe for you.'

Drew looked at Jamie for a long moment. 'Thanks, mate,' he said simply, and held his hand out.

Jennie began to tut as the two men shook hands. 'I couldn't *believe* it! I thought, Surely not *Drew*! I mean, what a crazy, irresponsible thing to do—to leave that much money lying around. Whatever were you thinking of?'

Shelley and Drew looked into each other's eyes and burst out laughing. 'Sorry,' said Drew as he drew her into his arms. 'I'm afraid I'm going to have to draw a veil over that! And while we're on the subject of veils…'

'*Yes?*' queried Jennie incredulously.

'Go away, Jennie,' he grumbled. 'I'm talking to Shelley.'

Shelley stared at him, oblivious to the fact that other people were present. 'Say that again.'

'What, veils?'

'What kind of veils?'

'Well, I'd sort of thought wedding veils.'

Her eyes were like saucers. 'You mean…marriage?'

He grinned. What had he said about passion dominating logic? 'I do. Oh, I do!'

And Shelley repeated those same words when they were married the following springtime—when the last of the winter chill had thawed away. The bride wore a pearl-white sheath sent with delight by Marco and his partner, and Shelley felt incandescent with joy as she made her wedding vows to the man she had loved for most of her life.

For two weeks they honeymooned almost exclusively at the Westward, barely setting foot outside the Lilac Suite—because, as Drew had told her, he had spent long enough imagining what it would be like to seduce her there. 'And the reality far exceeds the fantasy,' he had drawled.

In fact, she was of one mind with her husband on nearly everything, but especially when he looked at her with such tender love and smiled, and said that the best things in life were worth waiting for.

MILLS & BOON®

Makes any time special

Enjoy a romantic novel from
Mills & Boon®

Presents...™ *Enchanted*™ TEMPTATION.

Historical Romance™ ✚MEDICAL ROMANCE™

Copyright © Harlequin Enterprises Limited 1997
All rights reserved

COMING NEXT MONTH

MILLS & BOON®
Presents...™

MARRIAGE ULTIMATUM by *Lindsay Armstrong*
Neve couldn't work out why Rob Stowe was suddenly insisting upon marrying her, or whether she should even say 'yes' when the mother of his child was still so much in evidence!

MISTRESS BY ARRANGEMENT by *Helen Bianchin*
Nikos Alessandros needed a social hostess and Michelle needed a male companion to deter an unwanted suitor. A convenient affair—if they can keep their passions in check!

BARTALDI'S BRIDE by *Sara Craven*
Guido Bartaldi had obviously decided upon his reluctant ward as his wife. When Clare accepted a position with him she began to suspect that Guido had an entirely different set of intentions!

BOUGHT: ONE HUSBAND by *Diana Hamilton*
In her innocence Alissa offered to pay Jethro Cole to marry her, to comply with the conditions of her uncle's will. In fact Jethro was a millionaire intent on making Alissa his own.

Available from 5th November 1999

Available at most branches of WH Smith, Tesco, Martins, Borders, Easons, Volume One/James Thin and most good paperback bookshops

COMING NEXT MONTH

MILLS & BOON®

Presents...™

THE SOCIETY GROOM *by Mary Lyons*
(Society Weddings)

Once, they'd had a passionate affair. When they met again at a society wedding Olivia thought she'd lost all interest in Dominic FitzCharles—until he made a surprise announcement…

SLADE BARON'S BRIDE *by Sandra Marton*
(The Barons)

When Lara Stevens met Slade Baron an overnight flight delay led to a tempting invitation. Who would Lara hurt if she accepted? He wanted her and she wanted…a baby.

GIBSON'S GIRL *by Anne McAllister*

Gibson was fascinated by the shy and beautiful Chloe. Should he seduce her? Gib was tempted. Should she resist him? Chloe had to. Eventually it became a question of who was seducing whom!

MARRIAGE ON TRIAL *by Lee Wilkinson*

Elizabeth had insisted on an annulment - and disappeared from Quinn's life. Now he'd tracked her down and claimed she was still his wife. Did he really love her, or did he want revenge?

Available from 5th November 1999

Available at most branches of WH Smith, Tesco, Martins,
Borders, Easons, Volume One/James Thin
and most good paperback bookshops

MILLS & BOON®

MEDICAL
ROMANCE™

A FAMILIAR FEELING by Margaret Barker

Dr Caroline Bennett found working at the Chateau Clinique with Pierre, the boy she'd adored as a child, wasn't easy. It didn't help that his ex-wife was still around.

HEART IN HIDING by Jean Evans

Dr Holly Hunter needed respite, and the remote Scottish village was ideal. Until Callum McLoud turned up accusing her of treating his patients!

HIS MADE-TO-ORDER BRIDE by Jessica Matthews
Bachelor Doctors

Dr J.D. Berkely had a good job in ER, a delightful son Daniel, and a truly good friend in nurse Katie Alexander, so why would he need a wife?

A TIMELY AFFAIR by Helen Shelton

Dr Merrin Ryan sees that widowed Professor Neil McAlister needs nurturing and she falls in love! But Neil is aware that he could damage her career…

Available from 5th November 1999

Available at most branches of WH Smith, Tesco, Martins, Borders, Easons, Volume One/James Thin and most good paperback bookshops

This month's
irresistible novels from

TEMPTATION®

CONSTANT CRAVING by Tori Carrington

Eva Burgess was pregnant and she needed a husband—at least whilst she made a visit to her old-fashioned family! So she asked her new colleague Adam Grayson to play along. What she didn't know was that Adam was already working undercover—to investigate her!

STILL HITCHED, COWBOY by Leandra Logan

Mail Order Men

Letters arrived by the sackful in response to Matt Colter's ad for a wife, but he took his time choosing. And just as he'd settled on a candidate, his *first* wife, Jenna turned up. She was still sexy, still trouble. And much to Matt's annoyance—still hitched. *To him!*

STUCK WITH YOU by Vicki Lewis Thompson

Wyatt Logan was not at all pleased at being stuck in an empty house with a stranger—at least not at first. But trapped by the snow, he and Charity Webster were looking for ways to keep warm. And there was a lot to be said for body heat...

TANTALIZING by Lori Foster

Blaze

Josie Jackson didn't expect to like Nick Harris! She'd been set up by her sister, a situation that usually led to disaster. But instead of the world's most boring man, Josie found the sexiest man alive. And instead of a blind date from hell, she was heading for a night of passion.

9910

4 FREE

books and a surprise gift!

We would like to take this opportunity to thank you for reading this Mills & Boon® book by offering you the chance to take FOUR more specially selected titles from the Presents...™ series absolutely FREE! We're also making this offer to introduce you to the benefits of the Reader Service™—

- ★ FREE home delivery
- ★ FREE gifts and competitions
- ★ FREE monthly Newsletter
- ★ Exclusive Reader Service discounts
- ★ Books available before they're in the shops

Accepting these FREE books and gift places you under no obligation to buy, you may cancel at any time, even after receiving your free shipment. Simply complete your details below and return the entire page to the address below. *You don't even need a stamp!*

YES! Please send me 4 free Presents... books and a surprise gift. I understand that unless you hear from me, I will receive 6 superb new titles every month for just £2.40 each, postage and packing free. I am under no obligation to purchase any books and may cancel my subscription at any time. The free books and gift will be mine to keep in any case.

P9EA

Ms/Mrs/Miss/Mr ....Initials............................
                                          BLOCK CAPITALS PLEASE

Surname ....

Address ....

....

....Postcode................................

Send this whole page to:
UK: FREEPOST CN81, Croydon, CR9 3WZ
EIRE: PO Box 4546, Kilcock, County Kildare (stamp required)

Offer valid in UK and Eire only and not available to current Reader Service subscribers to this series. We reserve the right to refuse an application and applicants must be aged 18 years or over. Only one application per household. Terms and prices subject to change without notice. Offer expires 30th April 2000. As a result of this application, you may receive further offers from Harlequin Mills & Boon and other carefully selected companies. If you would prefer not to share in this opportunity please write to The Data Manager at the address above.

Mills & Boon is a registered trademark owned by Harlequin Mills & Boon Limited.
Presents... is being used as a trademark.

THE Regency COLLECTION

Where rogues find romance

Look out for the seventh volume in this limited collection of Regency Romances from Mills & Boon® in November.

Featuring:

The Cyprian's Sister
by Paula Marshall

and

A Compromised Lady
by Francesca Shaw

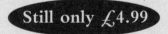

Still only £4.99

MILLS & BOON®

Makes any time special™

Available at most branches of WH Smith, Tesco, Martins, Borders, Easons, Volume One/James Thin and most good paperback bookshops